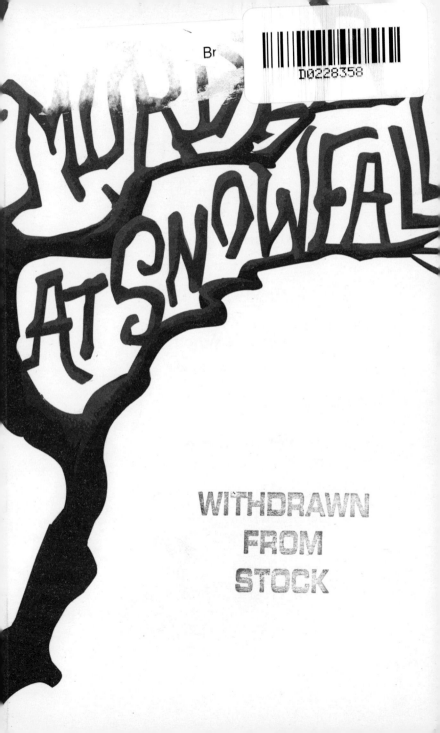

MURDER AT SNOWFALL

MURDER AT SNOWFALL

FLEUR HITCHCOCK

nosy
crow

First published in the UK in 2022 by Nosy Crow Ltd
The Crow's Nest, 14 Baden Place
Crosby Row, London, SE1 1YW, UK

Nosy Crow Eireann Ltd
44 Orchard Grove, Kenmare
Co Kerry, V93 FY22, Ireland

Nosy Crow and associated logos are trademarks and/or registered
trademarks of Nosy Crow Ltd

ISBN: 978 1 83994 590 8

A CIP catalogue record for this book is available from the British Library

Printed and bound in Great Britain by Clays Ltd, Elcograf S.p.A.
Typeset by Tiger Media

Papers used by Nosy Crow are made from wood grown in sustainable forests.

1 3 5 7 9 10 8 6 4 2

www.nosycrow.com

Prologue

"I bet there's a body in that." Lucas pulled his blazer tight around his chest. He pointed at the grey cabinet that had appeared in the lay-by a few days ago.

"Bet there isn't," I said, dragging my school skirt down to cover my frozen legs. "Why would anyone leave a body here?"

"Go on then, if you're so sure. Open it."

I stared at the cabinet. It was waist high, at an angle, propped against the skanky barbed-wire fence. Sleet flakes were settling on the metal. It was probably colder than we were. I touched it. It was.

"Ow!" I said. "That's frozen. If I'd left my hand there any longer, it would have got stuck."

"So?" he said.

I looked back at the cabinet. It was actually big enough to put a body in. "Suppose you're right?"

"But you said I couldn't possibly be. Go on. Open it."

I wish I hadn't. But I did.

Chapter I

The Christmas market's heaving. The people are so jam-packed that I've barely moved and I'd swear that if I took my feet off the ground I'd be carried all the way to the hot-dog stand without any effort. Behind me, the crowd surges forward and I lean into the tiny gap that's opened up in front of the man with the wooden neckties.

He glares at me; I'm very much in his space. Aaargh – I'm going to have to throw myself back into the people stream. I said I'd meet Mum at six, by the hot dogs. But there are two hot-dog stands and I don't know which one she meant, and there are about a billion tourists in between.

I'm really hungry so I hope she turns up soon. Hours ago, Mia and I shared a spiced apple juice and some overpriced roasted nuts. She ate most of them. I'm not that keen, to be honest. I'd rather have had a toffee apple thing. The nuts are now a distant memory and even though I can't hear it, I know my stomach's gone full cement mixer.

I catch a glimpse of a green quilted coat. "Mum!" I shout over the crowd, not that she's the faintest chance of hearing it. "Mum!"

She's looking around, but she can't see me. With a supreme and probably antisocial effort, I ram my way through the coats and bags and get to her just as she's heading off towards the abbey.

"Ruby!" she says. And she hugs me really hard, really close. For too long. We stand cheek to cheek, our hair mingling. Hers dark and mine mousey brown.

"What is it?" I mutter.

"Nothing, nothing, darling. I'm just happy to see you."

"Can we get something to eat?" I say, pushing

her away. "Can you be happy to see me in the hot-dog queue?"

She laughs and hugs me again, and we battle back through the crowds.

A moment later I'm burning my mouth on hot onions and I don't care. They're sliding down my chin on to my uniform. I gobble the whole thing while Mum laughs at me again and then, because she's my mum and she's prepared, she hands me a tissue to mop the oil and onion from my chin.

"Anything you particularly want to show me?" she says, and we link arms and batter our way around, buying Granny some soap and Paolo a lumpy sweater that Mum says he'll love, though I'm not so sure.

"What about Lucas?" she says as we drift to the edge of the market. I think of the gingerbread and candles and carved elf statues on offer. "I think he'd rather have some new headphones," I say. "Actually, please can you give him decent headphones? Or soundproofing? In fact, can you build him his own shed? Like, miles away?"

Mum would normally give me a disapproving glance, but instead she looks around, like she's expecting to see someone. "Headphones, you're right," she says, her gaze off somewhere over my shoulder. "I'll get Paolo to do some research."

"What is it, Mum? Are you OK?"

"Tell you in the car. It's time we went home," she says, taking my hand and tugging me away from the market.

"But you haven't even seen all the stands!" I point to the indoor market. "There's that whole bit over there."

"Come on, love, let's get home."

Letting go of my arm she stomps off towards Pulteney Bridge and I'm left standing, staring at her back and wondering what's going on.

We get to Great Pulteney Street before she starts talking.

"I'm sorry, Rube, but I've had an awful day," she says eventually. "I'm just not in the mood for the market."

"Is everyone all right? Is Granny OK?"

We stride past the huge houses; above us, coloured Christmas lights twinkle in the windows. Below, through half-closed shutters we can see into the basement flats. Kids doing their homework on kitchen tables, people chopping vegetables, one family putting decorations on their tree. It's Christmas perfect.

"No – nothing for you to worry about, everyone's fine. It's not that sort of awful day." We swing round the corner into the side street where she's parked the car. "It's about work."

The car's freezing. I clamp my hands between my knees and breathe on to them. Even after mum starts the engine and the fans come on full blast, all the heat does is clear a tiny arc of fog from the windscreen. Shivering, we thread our way on to the main road and in silence we creep up the hill in a slow worm of traffic. White Christmas lights on either side of us. A deer made out of stars galloping over a frail balcony. A tree trussed in festive cheer. One utterly out-of-place inflatable Santa bobbing on a roof top.

My mind wanders back to the market. I wonder if Mum'd like any of the things we saw. She didn't really react to anything, but then she wasn't concentrating.

Shame. I never know what to give her. She

buys everything she needs and she's picky about everything else. She complains about Granny being picky, but she's just as bad herself. I look across at her. By the brake lights of the car in front I can see that she's frowning. Lines on her forehead and her mouth clamped shut.

"So what is it, Mum?"

She's considering her answer. She probably doesn't want to worry me. Which is much more worrying than if she just spat it out. Eventually, she begins to talk. "I told you Dr Price didn't turn up yesterday? Well, he didn't turn up again today."

"Stressy."

"And when I got to the surgery this morning there'd been a fire."

"What? Had the whole place burned down? No way!"

"No, but it would have done; the fire brigade said it ran out of oxygen. It was just the office that got really badly damaged – but everything's covered in soot, unreadable or melted."

I try to picture the neat and tidy surgery blackened and burned. "Do you think Dr Price did it? Is he losing it?"

"No, it was a break-in. They came in through a window. We've still not heard from him. It's so … unlike him."

The traffic loosens and we speed up. Mum begins to talk again.

"We have digital records, of course. They're on an off-site server — but the computers have been trashed. The police were there all morning. I had to turn away patients, although the doctors saw as many as possible. I had no idea who was coming because the appointments are all computerised. It was awful."

"Not just you though? Jacqui and Oskar must have been there?"

"Oh, they were. It was all three of us trying to make it up as we went along — and then…"

"What?"

"Oh, nothing. It's silly."

"Mum?" I leave the word hanging in the air and we reach the top of the hill, where we wait behind a university bus.

"I'd swear I was followed back to my car."

"For real?"

I wait for her. She's thinking.

"I don't… I can't be sure, but you know, where I park my car – it's pretty tucked away? The chances of anyone else doing the same twists and turns to get there are like a hundred to one."

We crawl past the university, and streams of bikes, buses and cars flood the roads around us. Mum slows until we're at the top of Brassknocker Hill. We join the cars advancing in slow caterpillars down the slope. Ahead of us, the valley opens up into a few clusters of yellow lights, and a huge moon silhouettes the trees on the ridge opposite. She's right, the surgery is in the middle of a network of small roads and alleyways. But she could just be overthinking it.

The queue halts and we halt with it. To my left is a lay-by. On sunny days tourists stop and take pictures of the valley from here. It's famous and beautiful. It's also a place favoured by fly-tippers, and just now they've left a small filing cabinet thing and an armchair. Someone's graffiti-tagged the cabinet with a tiny white owl.

"Why would anyone follow you?"

She glances in her rear-view mirror. "I don't know."

"All the way to the actual car?" I ask.

She thinks about it.

"Actually, they didn't – because I stopped for a newspaper at the end of the parade."

"So they might not have been following you?"

"They might not," she says.

"So you might just be being paranoid?"

"I might," she laughs.

"Good," I say, and stare out at the blackness.

Chapter 2

When we get home I unlock the front door and we cram inside, dropping our bags and gluing ourselves to the big radiator in the kitchen. Lucas, my Step, is upstairs. I can hear him shouting at his computer. He talks to it more than he does to us.

"You must be frozen," says Mum, picking up a throw from the sofa and draping it over my shoulders. "I'm sorry about that car. It's so cold in the winter. I'll put the kettle on."

I take off my school shoes and bung them on the shoe rack. My feet are actually complete ice blocks now. If I moved my toes, they'd crunch.

"Tea?" says Mum. "Or do you need food? Although, I must just go to the loo." She charges upstairs to the bathroom.

With that, the landline starts to ring. It's probably a scam call. Deciding to chance it I hold the receiver to my ear. "Hello?"

"Hi, sweetie, is your mum there? It's Oskar." Oskar works with Mum at the surgery. He's lovely.

"Yeah, she's just in the bathroom. I'll—"

"Before you do, is she OK? It's just she was really rattled earlier. I wanted to check."

"I think so, although she thought someone followed her back to her car."

"Oh!" Oskar goes silent.

"What is it?"

"It's just… Oh, nothing. Paranoia probably."

"Not you as well!" I say. "What's going on?" I lift my right foot up so that it rests on the radiator. The burning heat is blissful.

He pauses for a long time. "Oskar?" I ask.

"I'm sorry, Rube, I know this sounds crazy, but I don't want to say it over the phone. Do you think Sally and Paolo would mind if I came round on

Sunday? There's just a load of stuff that doesn't quite make sense. I want to run it past your mum, face to face, before we go back in on Monday."

"I expect she'd love to see you, but she's here now," I say as Mum thumps down the stairs.

I hand Mum the phone and run upstairs to change into pyjamas and slippers. My room's next to Lucas's and I can hear the rumble of imaginary guns blasting imaginary foes through the wall. His room used to be the guest room. The house used to be quiet. And neat, and pretty but now … now there are bowls of congealing Weetabix on the stairs, socks on the bathroom floor, exploding backpacks blocking up the landing. It just isn't the same as it was.

I stuff my feet into the fleecy slippers that Granny gave me last Christmas.

For the moment, we tolerate each other. Or I tolerate him – I don't think he notices that I exist most of the time. I've been putting up with him for almost four months; before that we'd barely met. He lived with his mother in London. I hadn't really understood that if Paolo moved in with Mum, Lucas came too.

It never occurred to me that the room Granny often slept in would now be occupied by a stinky cyborg. But worse, in September, he started at my school. That first day was so weird. We ignored each other completely but then got back into Paolo's car at the end of the day and sat next to each other on the back seat.

In silence.

I shudder just to think about it.

We're in different year groups, thank goodness. He's a Year Eleven. A millennium away, but still.

Thing is, Mum and I have been on our own here for years. I was six when my dad left for a new life in Ireland. Since then he's had a new life in Portugal, Spain and France, and I think he's now back in Ireland. He's a complete loser. He'll send me an embarrassing jokey card at Christmas and an awful Christmas jumper with a reindeer on it or something. I don't miss him. Paolo and Mum began to date when I was in Year Five, and Paolo's much more fun.

I hear Mum's mobile ring downstairs.

They got married in the summer and now Lucas is officially what Mia calls my "Step". I've never had a sibling before. It's opened up a whole new world of complicated possibilities.

When I come back down, Mum's still on the landline.

"But, Oskar, why don't you just tell me over the phone?"

She listens to him and I stack breakfast plates into the dishwasher. Lucas could have done this. He really could.

"But…"

I pause.

"You think you know…"

She waits.

"For goodness' sake, tell me, Oskar. Don't be—"

She listens.

"Yeah, yeah – quite right. I think we're all rattled after today. It does make you imagine things. I imagined that someone followed me back to my car, but it was just nerves. Yeah … yup. See you Sunday. We'll see if we can put the whole thing to rights. Have a lovely evening, kiss kiss, bye now…"

Mum puts the phone down and picks up her mobile.

"Jacqui on one line and Oskar on the other. It's

really put the wind up us." She shivers. "I wish it wasn't the middle of winter."

"OK," I say, thinking of things that are normal. I switch on the radio – news burbles in the background – fill a pan with water and stick it on top of the stove. It hisses on the heat, and while Mum taps a message into her phone I empty a tin of tomatoes into another pan and bung two cloves of garlic and a swoosh of olive oil in with it. I would actually just eat the tomatoes heated up without the pasta. Or the pasta raw, or both of the above I am so hungry. But I'm trying to be helpful because I've never seen Mum so shaken. She's worse than when my dad left, or when Grandpa died.

Back then she retreated into romcoms. I wonder if she'll do the same this time. I'm not sure I can stand a back-to-back season of Hugh Grant.

I wander over to the piano and try a few notes of "Good Morning Baltimore" from *Hairspray*. It's the play we're doing this term and there are lots of songs. I know most of them from the film, but when Miss Johnson plays them on the piano there are notes and places where you're supposed to breathe that I'd never noticed before. I'm probably in the wrong key; I try and sing the chorus – but I can't do it without singing Tracy Turnblad's lines, which is fine because I'm the understudy for Tracy. So I kind of have to know it all.

Lulu who has the part will never be ill though. She's wanted to play Tracy Turnblad from the moment she stepped into school. I have too, but Lulu is so obviously desperate. And she's a Year Ten.

I have a tiny, short fantasy of Lulu getting suddenly struck down by a freak illness, or a bus, and immediately kill it dead. That way lies meanness – and I have vowed not to be mean. To anyone. Even Trixie Thompson, who deserves every scrap of meanness I can muster and has been perfectly cast as Amber Von Tussle. Miss Johnson must have put that in when she'd had a glass or two. But I guess Trixie would always see herself as a lead role, and she wouldn't want to play Tracy, so…

I must stop obsessing over it all. It's just a school play.

I stir the tomatoes.

But it would be brilliant if Lulu couldn't sing. She could get a tiny spot of laryngitis. Or just a sore throat.

Mum's standing in the hallway talking to Jacqui on her mobile. Jacqui works with Oskar and Mum at the Sundown Surgery. She's the other administrator. There are three doctors, a dentist and two receptionists. Mum does patient liaison, whatever that means.

Mum's talking in a hissy way, like when you don't want to be overheard, but I can hear individual words "Police … Dr Price … worried … crisis…"

Garibaldi the cat wanders in through the cat flap in the back door and looks up at me. I feed him. He's Paolo's and we're not best friends. Except that I'm the one who remembers that he needs food and so he doesn't poo on my bed. He only poos on Lucas's – so that's OK. He scarfs his saucer of disgusting meaty goo and wanders over to the sofa, shuffling among the cushions until he finds a comfortable position.

When she finishes her phone call, I pour Mum a glass of wine and she sits down next to Garibaldi in front of the telly and clicks over to the streaming services. She settles on *Love Actually*. Here we go then.

Paolo's motorbike growls in the yard outside. I turn back to the stove.

Paolo is kind and funny, and he cooks brilliantly. He works at the university wearing a white coat and looking in people's ears all day to see if they can move their eardrum. I know. Really specialised stuff. I think he should be up for a Nobel Prize but he laughed when I suggested it, saying that other scientists do much more groundbreaking work. I wonder if he was dull when he was a teenager. Perhaps one day, after metamorphosis, Lucas will turn from a gloomy caterpillar to a beautiful butterfly. Here's hoping.

I think Mum may indeed be paranoid, but I'm glad Paolo's back. He's so warm and generous. And I'm glad Lucas is upstairs shooting things. Even if he's completely useless. It feels better if we're all in one place. If I'm honest, Mum being rattled rattles me. And what did Oskar mean? And why couldn't he say it over the phone?

The front door swings open and Paolo comes in backward, kicking off his boots in the hall and throwing his gloves on the floor alongside.

"Oh, that was cold!" he bellows, launching his

jacket on to the hooks on the wall, where it misses and slides to the floor. "Hello, my lovelies! How was the market? Sally? How was your day? Ruby? Yours? And Lucas..."

"Good, thank you, Paolo. How was yours?" I ask, grinning. It's hard not to smile around him. He's infectiously cheerful.

"*Bene, bene*, sweetie. Guess what I did all day?"

"Look in people's ears?"

He ruffles my hair and kisses the top of my head. I turn back to the tomato sauce; he goes to sit next to Mum and they cuddle. I'm really fond of him but I still find it a bit weird. Uncomfortable, I suppose. For so many years I was the closest person to her – now I'm not so sure, and that intimacy between them is – eew.

I turn the radio over to a music channel.

Mum starts talking and through the music on the radio I hear her babbling about the surgery and the fire and everything.

Paolo makes soothing noises and Mum laughs and the low-level tension in the room starts to ease. Paolo takes over the cooking from me, peering sadly at my tomato sauce and adding a load of ingredients that bring it to life. A little later Lucas comes down to eat and mumbles a few words and goes back up to shoot things, and Mum and Paolo sit on the sofa to watch another romcom on Netflix. I stand in the kitchen feeling vaguely uneasy.

Later, just as I'm thinking about going to bed, Mum glances at her mobile.

"Oh! Another missed call from Jacqui. Do you think it's too late to call her back? Ten fifteen?"

"She'll still be awake," I say.

I hear the tones as she dials. "Jacqui?" she says, talking into her phone. "How are you?" I listen while she listens.

Jacqui's talking, and Mum's nodding her head. I pour milk into a pan and put it on the stove to warm and reach for chocolate powder.

"So it was a black car?"

I pause to listen.

"And it's been sitting out there on the road? This evening?"

Mum listens again.

"Are you on your own, Jacqui?"

Chapter 3

Mum and Paolo head over to Jacqui's and I go to bed, listening. Mostly, I hear the rumble of Lucas's guns and his occasional shouts of frustration. Then I hear him running from his bedroom, crashing both his door and the bathroom door open, and then comes the sound of loud peeing from a great height, the toilet flushing, thank goodness, and Lucas racing back into his room, doors slamming shut behind him.

I lie with my eyes open, thinking. I don't mean to think, it just keeps happening. I think about

Dr Price going missing, imagining all the places he might have gone. Perhaps he lives a double life, with another family, except he's not that sort of man. Then I think about Oskar. What did he want to say to Mum? I turn over and click my phone on. I could message him if I had his number – but then, all this has nothing to do with me.

I don't have his number. That's easy.

And then I think about Mum. About how worried she is.

Eventually, when I've properly fallen asleep, Mum and Paolo do that sneaking back into the house thing people do when they think they're being really quiet and they're not. I lie wide awake for a while after that.

At one point Mum comes in to sit at the end of my bed.

"S'all right, poppet," she says. "Go back to sleep."

I lie there for ages, waiting for her to go, and I fall asleep not sure if she's there or not.

It's completely dark when I hear someone go to the bathroom. I think it's Lucas, finally going to bed sometime in the early morning. I'm halfway asleep when it occurs to me that Lucas will have to wake up early; he has super-maths-for-clever-people at the uni in the morning. I get a spot of smug from the thought of him spending his sleep-deprived Saturday morning doing algebra while I pad around in my dressing gown. His fault for being so clever.

It's almost light when I wake up properly. My fingers squeak on the glass as I clear the condensation on the window.

It's a clear morning. Bright, cold. Shavings of frost on the leaves. A beautiful day.

Wearing my dressing gown I pad downstairs. The house is quiet. I open the French windows and step out on to frosty concrete. The big tank that collects rainwater from the roof has a solid sheet of ice across the top, creating a perfect Sylvanian skating rink.

Garibaldi sidles up to me. He's looking especially glossy this morning, as if he's spent the night eating small creatures and it agrees with him. If he has, he's still hungry. Closing the door, we go back into the kitchen and I feed him. He repays me by scratching the piano legs. "No, Garibaldi! No." But he looks at me with disdain and goes on scratching.

I have no authority.

Watery sounds come from Mum's bathroom, and then I hear Paolo's voice on the landing.

"You've got ten minutes. I'm going to do some work in the lab, get Sally a spare laptop. I'll take you on the bike."

Lucas rumbles from his bedroom. I can't decipher the words but he doesn't sound happy. A moment later and Paolo is singing in the kitchen and the coffee percolator is doing bubbly things.

Lucas appears, red-eyed and silent.

"Toast, Ruby?" asks Paolo.

"Please," I say, sitting alongside Lucas, who is stirring sugar into a cup of black coffee. He moves the toast around the plate, but doesn't eat it.

"Dad, do I have to go?" he asks, after picking the toast up twice, and replacing it twice.

Paolo stops spreading butter and, using the butter knife to emphasise his words, says, "Lucas. It is a privilege, not a burden."

Lucas lets out a long sigh.

My smug feeling wobbles. Perhaps this is the downside of being really smart. Other people thinking you're a genius and making you do things on Saturdays.

I reach across for the milk, and Lucas leans back out of the way. But he doesn't look at me or say anything to me. I stop feeling sorry for him.

"Why would they dismember the computers at Sally's work?" Paolo asks. He's obviously trying to engage Lucas in conversation.

And Lucas rises to the bait. Or at least, he lifts up his head and turns to his dad. "Hard drives, motherboards, PCUs – all full of precious metals, gold, platinum, neodymium."

"Neodymium, eh?" says Paolo, smiling.

"Or there was something on the hard drive they didn't want anyone to see," Lucas replies, "and they trashed the rest of the computers to—"

Mum thumps down the stairs holding her mobile to her ear.

"No! How awful!" she says. We all go quiet, listening for the little electronic voice at the other end. "Jacqui, calm down, it'll be OK," says Mum. "We'll come round to you." She closes her phone and glances up at me. "Get dressed, Rube, we're off."

"What?"

"Jacqui's had a break-in. She's all over the place."

"After we left?" says Paolo.

"I know." Mum shakes her head. "It's awful. Anyway, I can't leave you here alone, Ruby, not after yesterday. I wouldn't feel safe. So get dressed and we'll go and see Jacqui and pop into the market at the same time. Oh, and we'll drop Lucas on the way."

"But, Mum!"

"Ruby – just no. You're coming too."

Paolo puts four triangles of Marmite toast in front of Mum. She doesn't notice and I steal one. I feel I deserve it. I was going to swan about in PJs all day and now I have to go and see Jacqui and go vegetable shopping.

Mum doesn't notice that she's down to three triangles. I'm tempted to take a second piece even though I'm full. I slide closer to Mum's plate.

I hear a small intake of breath.

Lucas. He's watching my hand.

I can see thoughts moving behind his eyes. He doesn't speak.

"I wasn't going..." I say.

He raises his eyebrow and I feel the tiniest bit acknowledged.

As we're driving up the hill, Lucas gets a text to say his session is cancelled.

"Sorry, Lucas, can't run you back now, you'll have to come with us."

He sighs and stares out of the window and we head towards Jacqui's house.

We see the police cars immediately. Two of them, jammed into Jacqui's tiny drive.

"We've brought the coffee," says Mum, holding up a thermos to Jacqui as she answers the door.

"Sally, Ruby, oh — and Lucas. Let's go into the garden." Jacqui looks exhausted.

She guides us round the side of the house to a square of sunlight at the back and four white plastic chairs.

"What happened?" I ask. Lucas gets out his phone and leans against the wall; the rest of us sit down.

A policeman is examining the big sliding doors that give on to the garden and I can see two people moving about upstairs.

"Someone broke in around five, I think." Jacqui breathes heavily and stares at the back of her hand. "I was asleep, of course. But then I woke up and went for a pee — I thought the house was colder than normal, but I didn't go downstairs. Oh, Sally — there was someone in my house!"

Mum leans forward and gives her a hug. "I feel so guilty. They must have waited for us to go."

"Oh, don't be silly — you were here till three. I mean, how long could you hang around?"

"Still," says Mum. "I feel like the worst kind of friend."

"Look, Paolo offered to stay — and I sent you both off," she smiles. "It's on me."

"But are you all right?" I ask, trying to imagine what it would feel like to be burgled while you're sleeping.

Jacqui holds out her hand. It's shaking. She giggles. "It could just be the coffee. I've had a million cups since I found out."

"Well, do you want another one?" Mum asks, waving the thermos.

"Yeah." Jacqui shakes her head as if she can shake off the shivers. "It's all that's keeping me going."

Lucas looks up from his phone. "Did they take anything?" he asks, a millisecond before I was going to ask the same thing.

"I don't know," Jacqui says, watching Mum pour the coffee. "They made such a mess. But they didn't take the telly or anything obvious." She shivers again and pulls her cardigan closer across her chest. She's older than Mum, and her hands and neck are crisscrossed with tiny lines. The winter light is harsh, but I realise I've never seen her without make-up before. She usually presents a glossy, groomed appearance. Probably makes it easier to deal with tricky patients. Today she looks about twenty years older. Faded. Tired.

There's a long silence and then Mum says, "What a week. Dr Price missing, the surgery vandalised, and now this."

"They're related?" I ask.

Lucas looks at me sideways.

Jacqui takes a long time to reply. "You'd think so, wouldn't you? Too much of a coincidence otherwise."

A police officer comes out to Jacqui. She introduces herself as Detective Sergeant Afolabi.

She's smiley but looks at us doubtfully, like she wonders why we're all there. Mum and I pretend to be really interested in a dead plant in the corner of the garden. It's just about the only plant. Lucas keeps his eyes on his phone. Naturally, I'm listening to the conversation.

"So apart from your laptop, which you think your son – er – Anthony, has, is there anything else that you can see is missing or disturbed?"

"My jewellery's all upstairs in my room – and they didn't…" Jacqui goes inside with the police officer and points to things. I watch her through the big sliding doors. She looks very nervous. I guess she would be.

"Poor thing," says Mum. And then, "Poor thing," again.

Jacqui comes back out alone, this time with a blanket over her shoulders. "I hate this. I feel violated. Utterly invaded. I'd like to go as far away as possible. Or stay in a hotel – but I can't afford it," she says.

"You could stay with us…" Mum begins, and I glare at her.

Lucas glances up, panic in his eyes.

There is no spare bedroom in our house. Lucas sleeps in it and it would mean him and me sharing, which is not going to happen no matter how much of a friend Jacqui is.

"Don't be silly." Jacqui winks at me and glances over to Lucas. "You can't ask them to share. Imagine!" she laughs.

"You could stay with Granny," I say.

Mum and Jacqui both laugh at this.

"She could," I say.

"It's true." Mum nods. "And Granny would love it, but I'm not sure Jacqui would. Couldn't you get anyone to stay with you? How about Anthony?"

Anthony is Jacqui's son. I think of him as a formaldehyde being that crawled out of a bottle. Lucas is pale and screen-addicted, but I don't think Anthony has ever seen the light. He could actually be a vampire or an alien. His skin is so white, it's blue. I've only met him a few times. He's perfectly polite although he looks at you for slightly too long and stands slightly too close. But he's Jacqui's son; I don't think she thinks he's weird.

Jacqui shakes her head. "No — poor love, he's working on hush-hush cyber business, illegal phone-tappers and whatnot. He's got a lot on at the moment." She twists her rings on her fingers. "Bless him, and he's got some extra work from Seb, resetting electronics on the security gates at the park."

"Why can't you stay with Sebastian?" asks Mum. "After all, you'll be married in a couple of weeks."

Jacqui is marrying this incredibly posh man who owns a safari park. Sebastian Duncan. I don't know him well, but Mum says he's gorgeous and warm and perfect for Jacqui.

Jacqui smiles. Rubbing her chin as if she's thinking.

"Maybe I'll stay with him tonight, but it's too far to get to work – even the driveway takes ten minutes. That's why I'm transferring to the other surgery." Jacqui glances at her phone. "But you guys must go – don't hang around here. I'll see you on Monday."

Mum hugs her, then it's my turn. Her perfume catches in my throat as she pulls me close and I have to turn away, bumping into Lucas, who is already backing across the lawn. If he goes on living with us, he's going to have to get used to Jacqui. And her chemical hugs.

She stands outside the front door as we drive away. She shivers and pulls the cuffs down on her cardigan. She looks very small.

Chapter 4

We go to the Green Park market. Mum fills up with bags of vegetables that she hopes she can get me and Lucas to eat. Kale, beetroot and a thing that looks like it comes from space that she assures me is edible. "Kohlrabi," she announces. "Paolo can make it into something delicious."

Lucas trails behind us, unaware that he's swinging the heavy bags into people's legs. I'm trying to work out how to say something when Mum hands him a small meat pie and takes the bags off him.

He grunts and bites his way through it in three

massive chomps.

Gross.

And I was just wondering if he was wondering about everything that's been going on.

Maybe not.

Piling back into the car, we set off again, and I can tell that Mum's not concentrating. We narrowly miss a bus on Bathwick Hill and she goes far too close to a bollard by the university. We drive past our turning and carry on up the hill to Granny's house on the edge of the village.

There's a tiny lay-by outside Granny's; the owl tagger's been here too. The telephone connection box has a neat little owl over the keyhole. Nice.

Granny's at the window, waiting for us. Mum sighs and pulls over. She steps out of the car and waves, and I roll across her seat grabbing one of the bags of veg on my way. Lucas opens his door and clambers out like some kind of awkward spider. By the time I'm out, Granny is standing in the open door, pulling Mum down for a kiss and shooing her through the house.

I follow, taking a last deep breath of the fresh outdoor air before going inside into the sweltering atmosphere of Granny's superheated house. The wall of doggy fug greets me before I trip over her massive collection of walking aids that she needed when she had a hip operation and hangs on to "just in case".

As I step around a wheeled frame, an overweight Labrador barrels out from the front room, chucks himself at my legs and brings down an avalanche of walking sticks.

"Donald!" shouts Granny.

"Hello, disgusting dog," I say, rubbing his neck and piling all the sticks back against the wall. He sniffs all around me and then, realising that I'm only carrying vegetables, disappears back into the front room.

Behind me, Lucas closes the front door. I'm surprised he came in, to be honest.

From the kitchen I hear Granny remarking on everything that Mum's bought.

"That's a very large turnip. I don't need all that."

"Well, we can cut it in half if you like."

"Call that a lettuce?"

Mum doesn't answer.

"I wanted one chop, not two. I can only eat one."

"Stick the other one in the freezer."

Granny tuts, and I hear the rustle as she turns to her cache of pre-loved plastic bags.

"Hi, Granny," I say, putting a bag of potatoes on her table. "How many of these do you want?"

"Ooh, look at you!" she says, bustling towards me and grabbing me in a wiry hug. "How are you, darling?"

"All good," I say. "How are you?"

"Oh – and gorgeous Lucas too!" She motors towards him, hugging him hard, her head somewhere in the middle of his stomach.

"How are you, Polly?" he mumbles, wondering what to do with his arms and lowering them so that they almost touch Granny's shoulders, but not quite. I stare as a full-on blush races up his neck.

"All the better for seeing you, lovely boy. Toast and honey?"

It's all so normal that when we get back home I've almost forgotten about the weird things happening at the surgery, and I grab a sandwich and go up to my room. I message Mia, trying to explain everything. But before I've sent the second message, she videocalls me back.

"What. Is. Going. On?" she says.

I put the phone on speakerphone and balance it on the windowsill so that I can eat my sandwich at the same time as talking.

"So is your mum going to work still? Or what?"

"Yeah, she is. Or will be, on Monday."

"And the doctor – is he still missing?"

"He is. Not a squeak from him as far as I know."

"That is so spooky!"

"And Oskar – you know, the guy with the weeny goatee – he said something … although, he didn't."

"What do you mean?"

"I don't know, but Jacqui's house got broken into. She looked really, like, old."

Mia rolls her eyes at me. "That's cos she is – der! What about your Step – what's he doing?"

"He's just in his room now," I hiss, jabbing the speakerphone button and hoping that he's got his headphones on. "He hasn't said anything. I didn't think he'd even noticed that Mum's all – you know, worried. We took him to Jacqui's house and he just stared at his phone – but he was kind of maybe listening. You should have seen him at Granny's. She gave him a huge hug and he was so embarrassed."

"Oooh. Has he got a girlfriend?"

"What – Lucas? You're joking. All his friends are, like, nerds. They come and eat pizza and make jokes about orcs."

Downstairs, Paolo gets out his guitar. He's getting better. I recognise the chords; it's a song he and the other ancient people in his band have been playing. Luckily they're all terrible and they have no intention of performing. He's made that clear. It's just for fun. I wouldn't tell him, but I'd love to have a go at singing with them. Even the awful songs they choose would be fun.

"So have you learned all the words?" I ask.

"No – have you?" she laughs. "Although I will tomorrow, I promise. Anyway, are you still on for the party?" It's Mia's birthday party just before Christmas.

"Of course. But it's not for ages, is it?"

"You cannot overthink these things. Especially in my house. I've got these chill lights we can put up in the garden, and Dad says we can use the gazebo thing from his work, so we can have a tent out there, which'll be cool because the house is –

well, meh."

Mia's mum and dad are separated too, but she lives with her dad and he's got the saddest furniture. Their house smells of dog too, but not like Granny's. Theirs is pig-farm dog smell, whereas Granny's is just farty Labrador.

"Ace," I say. "So we'll be in the garden?"

"Yeah. Hope it snows."

"That would be magic."

We're comparing notes on whether you could live on frozen peas or baked beans forever when the doorbell rings.

I'm nosy, so I go downstairs. I carry some dirty socks – they were all I could find as an excuse – and bung them in the washing machine to look busy. Two people come into the house. One is the detective who was at Jacqui's house, but I've not seen her male colleague before. They look tired, or maybe annoyed. Perhaps they'd been hoping to do their Christmas shopping today – after all, there are only twenty-four shopping days to Christmas.

"Hello, I'm DS Afolabi, and this is DS Green. Can we sit down somewhere?" She takes the lead. I open the fridge and stare inside while listening.

"So, Dr Price. He's still missing."

"It's been two days now," says Mum. "Actually three. We're really worried."

I turn around, my back to the counter, and eat a yoghurt as slowly as I dare. Our house is what they call open plan – you can wander from one room into another without going through any doors. It's great if you don't want privacy.

DS Afolabi writes something in a notebook she takes from her jacket pocket. "Yes, so we just wondered if the doctor had been acting normally? Strangely? Do you think this is in character?"

Mum's smiling. "Oh no, not at all, Dr Price is the most efficient and hard-working GP I've ever known. Except for his wife, of course, Dr Anna Radcliffe. She's incredible. They've given their all to the local community, and I don't remember him ever taking a day off."

DS Afolabi writes Mum's answer in her book. Her colleague gets up from the sofa and checks out the shelves that line the walls. He looks at photos, the CD collection, the spines of books. It feels vaguely invasive.

Feet sound on the stairs and Lucas swings round

into the kitchen. He too puts some socks in the washing machine and then opens the fridge.

"And you last saw him when – Wednesday?"

"That's right. I left and he stayed. He was going to walk home, he said. To clear his head. It was late because I had to pick Ruby up from a basketball match – they didn't get back until seven – and I didn't want her to wait for a bus, so I sorted out the rota for the next day."

Lucas takes a load of jars from the fridge and examines them, like a scientist looking at specimens. He's welcome to the lone floating gherkin. It's been there for years.

"So you'd normally leave at...?"

I look back towards the sofa.

"Six – six fifteen."

DS Afolabi scribbles it in her book. Her fingers are small and manicured, and she draws smiley hearts and faces in the margins. Is she bored? "How was he? How did he seem?"

Mum bites her lip and stares out the window into the sunlit garden. "Normal – really normal. Busy, stressed, checking out things from drug companies, looking for patient records, not finding them."

"Any one in particular?"

Mum shakes her head. "No, it's always like that. And of course it's winter, so more people, more viruses, you know."

Alongside me, Lucas leans against the counter. He peels the top from a yoghurt, drops it and pours the yoghurt into his mouth. And then he stays there, holding the empty yoghurt pot, listening.

"So do you still have paper records, or are they all digital now?"

"They're all digital and have been for years. But there are prescriptions and notes and invoices. Current things that haven't been put on file. We still have accounts like any other business."

"And those?"

"All gone. Blood tests, all sort of things like that. All in that fire. There wasn't even a Post-it note left. Do you think it's connected to his disappearance? Poor Anna, she must be worried sick."

"S'all connected," mutters Lucas.

"Sorry?" I say.

But he chucks his empty yoghurt pot at the sink and lopes back off upstairs. I'm still wondering if I heard it right when DS Afolabi stands up, picking cat hairs from her neat navy-blue trousers.

"We'll hope to find Dr Price and then things will be clearer. Any information – if you'd let us know." She hands Mum a card and walks to the door.

"Er, Mum," I say. "What about last night?"

Mum frowns.

"You know, you said you were followed."

"Oh – I don't know,"

"Followed?" DS Afolabi pauses.

"It was nothing – honestly. I was jumpy, you know…"

DS Afolabi looks to Mum and then back to me. "Well, if there is anything…"

"No," says Mum. "Nothing."

DS Green, who's examining Paolo's Latin jazz collection, hurriedly follows DS Afolabi to the door and they let themselves out.

We stand for a moment listening for the sound of their car starting. I look across at Mum. Her lip wobbles, barely at all, but just enough for me to see. Oh no, I wanted to go upstairs and find out what Lucas meant but… "Tell you what," I say. "I'll put the kettle on."

Chapter 5

Later on, I catch Lucas on his way back to his room from the kitchen. If I'm honest, I've been sitting inside my bedroom door waiting to spring on him, so I suspect I come over a bit more kangaroo than I intended.

"What?" he jumps, slopping chocolate milk over the side of the bowl he's clutching, leaving a pool on the landing carpet.

I almost run straight to the bathroom for some loo paper and start mopping it up, but remember that I have only this one chance before he's locked in deadly combat for the rest of the evening. "What did you mean? It's connected?"

He stares at me. I can't work out if he's thinking I'm incredibly stupid, or irritating, or perhaps he's not thinking anything at all. Eventually, he frowns. "The doctor person, the surgery fire, the break-in — all connected. Coincidences don't happen — there's a reason."

"What?"

He shrugs. "Dunno. Can I go now?"

I stand back, he brushes past, and the moment he's gone I run for the loo paper.

Later, when Mum's in the bath, I flick through her phone. It feels like stealing, but I'm only looking for Oskar's number. It's there in the call history and I copy it down, taking it back up to my room.

And then I stare at the piece of paper for an age.

In the end, I videocall Mia.

"What's happened?" she asks.

"Police, but they didn't say anything. Mia, do you think it would be weird if I rang Oskar? You know, the bloke at the surgery who works with Mum and Jacqui."

She's silent for a while. "A bit weird. Why would you?"

"Because he has suspicions. Or something. And I do too. And I'd like to know what's going on." I drop my voice to a whisper. "And the Step thinks it's all connected. So it's not just me."

Mia sits back. Eyebrows making an escape into her hairline. "Ring him then. Go on."

But I don't. I go to bed and worry about whether or not to ring him all night until it's Sunday, which is the day he's coming round anyway.

Every week Sunday is the very best until four o'clock when it becomes the very worst.

Only because school crashes into Sunday night no matter how hard I try and keep it back. It's not that I hate school. It's more that I'm not very good at it. Or it wasn't built for me. I just get bored. So bored it hurts and I lose interest. At primary it was OK because we did lots of immersive, interactive things, but sitting in front of a whiteboard all day and copying things down goes straight past me. I'm dyslexic, so that might possibly be why.

Or it could just be that my school is rubbish.

Either way, I do feel that I have to work harder than

everyone else to reach the same point, and people like Trixie and Euan Henderson have spotted it. Euan looks at me sadly, like I'm a broken-winged bird or something. Trixie just gets her knife out and gives me a prod. Not her real knife, her word knife. I can't come back at her snarky comments; I'm not quick enough. Mia's good though. She often tells me what to say, or tells me to walk away from it, which is what I'm trying to do these days. After all, as she says, we're not eight any more.

Sunday mornings are usually good. Paolo cooks a full English/Italian breakfast – delicious – and he makes mochas with frothy milk and I love it. This Sunday is almost the same as usual. But there's something in the air. Mum keeps on getting up and down, and Paolo notices.

"A walk?" says Paolo.

"Oh yes," says Mum. "Ruby? Join us? Oskar's coming round later on the bus."

I look out of the window. The sky is flat grey. Almost yellow. Like it could snow. I could go for a walk, or I could snuggle down with Netflix and a packet of crisps that I happen to know has fallen down behind the pasta at the back of the cupboard and that Lucas hasn't spotted.

But Mum's phone rings and it's Jacqui.

Mum listens for a moment and then says, "Both come round, why don't you? Oskar will be here around four. D'you know what? I'll make a cake."

So the afternoon disappears. Paolo goes for a walk on his own listening to some painful jazz through his headphones. Mum makes the cake. I watch Netflix in my room with half an ear out for the doorbell. Lucas doesn't make a cake or go for a walk. He swears at his computer and shoots life forms with green blood.

It's easy to tell when they arrive. Bursts of laughter come from downstairs and I wander down to the fridge and examine the dates on the yoghurts. I want to be there if there's a chance to talk to Oskar without Mum. Behind me, Jacqui's raucous laugh fills the space and Mum joins in. Jacqui's made up this time and much more like the person I've known all my life. Funny, noisy, shiny. Her yellow-blonde hair swept into curls, her lips red. Gold dangling from her wrists and fingers. She's wearing a faux leopard-skin coat and shoes with gold chains on them. Behind her is Oskar. He's young. So much younger than Mum and Jacqui, and he looks slightly uncomfortable bumbling along in Jacqui's wake. He wears funky hand-knits that he must find in second-hand shops. The way he dresses is the exact opposite of Jacqui. He's kind of cool, and I know he likes music and goes to gigs all the time because Mum talks about it with Paolo.

"How are you?" Mum asks Jacqui.

Jacqui lets out a long sigh. "Well, after the police left, I tidied up. Still couldn't find anything missing, so I got on with my place settings for the wedding." She gives Mum a significant look. She and Sebastian are getting married a week on Friday. I wonder if she's asked Oskar to the wedding because he's staring out of the window in a fixed and very uncomfortable way. "And then I had a normal sort of evening, you know, watched a rerun of *Amazing Spaces* and ate chocolate to make myself feel better."

I get out a tray and load it with mugs and plates, and some dainty forks that someone gave Mum and Paolo as a wedding present. Mum and Jacqui go to the sofa in the sitting room and I beam a big smile at Oskar.

"How are you, Ruby?" he says, wandering over. "Can I help?"

"Hi, Oskar, What did— Oh!"

Lucas crashes in behind me, dropping three bowls into the sink and opening the fridge in a single movement. He takes the orange juice from the door and empties a huge glug of it into his mouth.

Oskar winces and Lucas stops, holding the carton in mid-air. "Sorry," he says. "Did you want some?"

I shake my head and pour milk into a jug. "What was I asking? Oh yes." I drop my voice to a whisper. Lucas leans in too. "What did you want to say to Mum that you didn't want to say over the phone?"

Oskar glances over to Mum and Jacqui, who are examining table plans for the wedding on Jacqui's phone, and turns his back on them. I notice how tired he looks, actually grey, and for a second I'm just watching his mouth move before I understand what he's saying.

"It's so weird. I've been thinking about it ever since Friday and now I'm sure Dr Price had spotted something in the records or the letters that didn't add up, like someone's done something— Oh, Jacqui!"

Jacqui swoops past us in the kitchen, heading for Mum's cake. "But, Sally, what a marvel is this? Proper tempered chocolate too!" She scrapes a painted fingernail around the bottom of the cake, scooping up a single misplaced blob and landing it on her tongue.

Oskar coughs. Mum laughs and sweeps Oskar and Jacqui and the cake into the sitting room.

"What *about* Dr Price?" mutters Lucas. "Where's he gone?"

"Perhaps he confronted someone about … you know, they had a fight or something," I say, surprised that Lucas is interested enough to remember the doctor's name.

"What?" says Lucas. "And he's lying beaten up somewhere?"

"Maybe," I say. "Maybe he's being held at gunpoint by a patient—"

"Shh, listen." Lucas holds up his hand and we both freeze to hear.

"I reckon it's a burglar – after drugs, or prescriptions," Jacqui says, her voice cutting through everyone else's. "That stuff happens all the time, doesn't it?"

Mum starts talking about a break-in at another practice over in Salisbury.

"No, no, it doesn't make sense," says Oskar. "You'd go to a pharmacy, not a surgery for drugs. And if you were after precious metals you'd steal catalytic converters, not a load of office equipment."

I step out of the kitchen so that I can see them. Oskar looks really worried.

"Oh, I don't know," says Jacqui relaxing back on to the sofa. "Let's leave it to the police, shall we?" She helps herself to another slice of Mum's cake. "Now, you two chickens in the kitchen. Tell us about *Hairspray*. Sing us a number – I'm so looking forward to it."

Monday. I hate Mondays. Lucas and I wait for the bus in silence. It's like that moment in the kitchen yesterday has vanished, but I want to know what he thinks has happened. He obviously isn't buying into the precious metal thing or the stolen prescription thing, but I just can't quite think of a way of getting past his earbuds.

"Lucas?" I say.

He doesn't even move his head.

I try again. "Lucas!"

"What?" he snaps back at me.

"What did you mean yesterday? About Dr Price. And what did you think about what Oskar said?"

Lucas gazes into the distance. "Dunno, it's too early in the morning." He shrugs and puts his earbuds back in.

I would kick him if I didn't think Mum would get to hear about it.

The bus arrives and we sit at opposite ends, both turning to our phones for friendship. I footle through my messages. Some people are already in school. It looks as if the scuzzy changing rooms have had a cheap makeover at the weekend. They're now seasick blue instead of vomit green. By tonight they'll be covered in graffiti.

Outside the bus, there are pretty spider's webs with frost jewels hanging in the hedge, and the big rugby pitch on the left has a small frozen lake at the side. I shiver. I probably should have brought a coat. But I always feel so awkward in a coat. None of the cool kids wear coats. Unless they're like five-hundred-pound coats from some swish place in London.

The bus pulls in to school and we all scrabble to escape the fumes. I don't know who does the acid farts every morning, but someone on that bus does and it's enough to make you throw up.

I get to tutor – a moment late, but ahead of most of the others, and check out my phone again before I bury it in my bag. Mum's sent a message on the family group – she can't pick us up tonight. We've both got *Hairspray* rehearsals. Why is Lucas doing the play? I don't know. If you were to pick a Year Eleven to play a part in a musical, it wouldn't be him. I didn't even know he was doing it until I saw him at the first rehearsal, hiding behind the curtains like he wasn't really there.

He's actually playing Corny Collins – it's a proper part. He's supposed to be a hunk, and a good dancer. Two descriptions that land badly on Lucas.

It's a total gamble. I overheard Mum and Paolo talking about it. They're hoping something extraordinary will happen and he'll cast off his shyness and be brilliant. I'm hoping that he pulls out and that Euan Henderson takes over, because he can act.

I don't know what possessed them to cast Lucas.

Then Mrs Lovatt comes in and someone tips their pencil case off the back of the desk.

The rehearsal is somewhere between tedious and embarrassing. Two people have forgotten to come but we manage to get through the dance sequences without anyone breaking a limb. It's lacklustre until Desta in Year Eleven who is playing Motormouth Maybelle does a blistering performance of "I Know Where I've Been" and we all melt.

Things improve after that. People make more of an effort, although watching Lucas try to dance is painful and he obviously hasn't learned his part.

Trixie says something to Siobhan standing beside her. They both giggle.

"It's only two weeks or so till the performance," whispers Mia, and I glance at Miss Johnson sitting behind the piano and I can see the fear in her eyes.

"He can sing though," I say. It's true. Lucas can sing. It's just all the other things he's going to have to do are so woeful.

I look at Lucas's back as he goes off to sit next to one of his friends. The friend says something and they laugh together. It might be the first time I've ever seen him smile.

But he is terrible.

I feel very slightly smug that, for once, I might possibly be better at something than Lucas.

"Right, everyone!" Miss Johnson claps her hands together. We gather round, and she gazes at the floor. "So – two weeks Wednesday. That's less than fourteen days before the dress rehearsal. In that time you all need to learn ALL the words to your songs – all the movements in your dances, all your spoken script, which isn't that much. I know it's hard to do that kind of thing on your own, so I recommend that you buddy up with other people who are in the scenes you're in..." Everyone starts talking at once. "Or, failing that – just people who live near you." She looks directly at me, and then at Lucas. "OK?"

Chapter 6

We meet outside. It's dark and it's really cold, but the next bus into town is in twenty-five minutes, and behind us I can hear the caretaker locking up the building. "Walk into town and then catch a bus out?" I say to Lucas, who shrugs his backpack higher and lets out a long sigh.

"Why don't we walk home," he says. "We'll have to go up Winsley Hill, but honestly, I reckon it'll take about the same amount of time."

"In these?" I look down at my shoes. They're thin court shoes that are good for dancing, but not blundering down paths in the dark.

"Got your PE kit?" he says.

He has a point and I change my courts for a pair of toxic running shoes with extra socks.

The path along the main road is well lit, and anyway, I'm not worried about walking in the dark – where we live, it's always been dark at night. It's not that I can actually see more, it's maybe that I'm better at finding my way using my feet and worrying less about my eyes.

We don't talk to each other, and I'm aware that Lucas is wearing headphones. Good, that avoids embarrassing chat about *Hairspray*, although I'd still like to have a proper discussion about the break-ins and Dr Price. But maybe now isn't the time.

We get to the corner of a field where a footpath crosses behind a signpost. The owl tagger's been here too. This time they placed it neatly on the corner.

It's as if they don't want their graffiti to be noticed. They're shy about it.

"Here?" I say, swinging into the field and not giving him a chance to answer. I know it's the best way; I walked down here last term a few times. It was summer then. Mia came. We walked so that we could go swimming in the river, except someone said it was full of sewage so we sat on the side and watched everyone else go in before catching a bus home. I like swimming in the river. But further upstream. Not by the weir. It's too full of people having stinky barbecues and scattering cans everywhere. Sometimes Paolo goes down at first light; he cycles and sometimes I go too. It's magic then. Kingfishers and herons and no people.

We walk on.

The best swimming is up in the pool behind Granny's. It's a new private swimming club but she pretends to be a member and no one's brave enough to challenge her. We go when it's almost dark, me and Granny, over the barbed-wire fence and into the warm water.

I shiver. I could do with warm water now. My hands are so cold I can't feel them.

We leave the light behind us and stumble over the field. Under my feet the tussocks crunch. Frost. I sense that Lucas is slowing down, probably because he's less sure of the ground, so I take out my phone and turn the torch on. The ground's silver. Or rather the grass is. Long glittering spikes all around us. Magic. Lucas catches up with me.

"Thanks," he mutters.

"'K," I say, smiling to myself. I think that's the first time he's ever said thanks. Perhaps when we get home I should try to get him dancing.

I imagine the scenes.

"Do you want to practise some songs from the show?" I suggest. "No one would be able to hear us."

"Let's not," he says.

"'K," I say.

I tried.

"What do you think's happened?"

He catches up with me. "At the surgery?"

"Yup."

He's silent for a while and we pick our way across the field with the distant serenade of a police siren.

"I reckon Dr Price is the key to the whole thing."

"But he's missing."

"That, indeed, is the problem."

"So you haven't a clue?"

"Precisely," he answers, and I can hear the smile in his voice.

We reach the end of the field and slip along the wall towards Brassknocker Hill. There's a house on the right, all cosy and warm. In front, a steady stream of cars.

"We could go straight over and down the field on the other side. It takes you down to the main road and then there'd be a stretch along the canal."

Lucas gets his phone out and looks at the map. "I've done the road before," he says. "Less slippery."

I look down at my trainers and although there's every chance we'll get run over on the road, I suppose it's better than breaking our necks on the steep slope of the footpath. "Or we could go down the first bit, where there's a verge, and then cut through the sheep field to the lane at the bottom."

"Let's go to the lay-by, cut down that way," he says.

"If we're not killed before we get there," I say, crossing the road and stepping on to the grassy verge.

The lights slide past, flashing on to the stone wall to my left, lighting up my shoes, time after time. The grass verge runs out and we have to walk on the road itself.

Toooot!

I ignore it.

Two more cars pass us, the second one beeping its horn, and I immediately regret the plan. We're wearing black; this is just stupid. "We should go back up to the footpath. We'll be killed here."

"What?" shouts Lucas.

"We should turn round!" I shout.

But he can't hear me.

"We should go back up, take the footpath. This is just lethal." The cars swing past, long streams of them, one after another. I'm about to start walking back up when there's a break in the traffic. I run down to the lay-by halfway down the hill. As I run, something twinkles in the headlights. I lean down to pick it up. It's embedded in the mud thrown up by the cars. It's hard and cold, but I can't hang around inspecting it so I pluck it out and bung it in my pocket and swoop on down to the lay-by. I make it before the first car.

Lucas arrives by my side a moment later.

Alongside us is the grey filing cabinet that I noticed on Friday, although the armchair's gone.

Next to the box, there's a new gate, quite small.

"I reckon if we climb over that we can get down to the bottom of the field without breaking anything."

"Is that snow?" he asks. Something's slanting in the headlamps.

I feel my face. It's so cold I hadn't noticed, but I've definitely got tiny balls of ice on my eyelids.

"Could be." I stuff my hands under my armpits to thaw. The only bit of me that's at all warm is my feet. "Which way? Up or down there?" I look over the fence towards the farm below.

"I bet there's a body in that." Lucas pulls his blazer tight around his chest. He points at the grey cabinet.

"Bet there isn't," I say, dragging my school skirt down to cover my frozen legs. "Why would anyone leave a body here?"

"Go on then, if you're so sure. Open it."

I stare at the cabinet. It's waist high, at an angle, propped against the skanky barbed-wire fence. Sleet flakes are settling on the metal. It's probably colder than we are. I touch it. It is.

"Ow!" I say. "That's frozen. If I'd left my hand there any longer, it would have got stuck."

"So?" he says.

I look back at the cabinet. It's actually big enough to put a body in. "Suppose you're right?"

"But you said I couldn't possibly be. Go on. Open it."

The traffic goes quiet. For a full couple of minutes, no cars pass up or down the hill.

I wouldn't open it. Not normally, but I wonder if he's thinking what I'm thinking and this is the only chance we're ever going to have. I'm certainly never walking down this bit of road again.

I put my hand out. The cabinet has a handle on the back. It looks like one of those old-fashioned twisty ones.

"OK," I say. "Although if there is a body, you'll have to ring the police – yeah?"

"Yup," he says. "Get on with it. Before we die of hypothermia."

I lean over the top and turn the handle.

I don't know what I'm expecting, but the moment I turn it and the door swings open I can't stop whatever it is from falling out on to the frozen grass.

"Oh!" I jump back.

Lucas beams his phone torch on to the thing

that's slumped behind the box.
   It's a black plastic bag.
   Heavy.
   Person-shaped.

Chapter 7

Paolo manages to get to us before the police. He's on his bike, but just having him there makes us warmer.

"My poor loves," he says, holding us together in an awkward embrace. "What is it? Do you think it's...?"

We are clustered at the other end of the lay-by, I shine my phone torch at the black plastic. "What do you think?"

"It's probably nothing," he says. "This just may be a very clever way of you two getting a lift home in a police car, eh?"

I laugh in spite of myself, but the plastic bag is stretched around an outline that looks all too human.

I swing my torch along the lay-by. The light catches on a can and a couple of crisp bags. "I'll pick them up," says Paolo.

"D'you think you should, Pa?" says Lucas. "If it is a body – then…"

"Better not then," Paolo replies.

And we wait.

It takes almost an hour for the police to arrive.

"Christmas market," they say in explanation. I don't care. I just want to sit in the police car and see if my fingers are still attached to my hands. Once again there are two police officers, and while we sit in the car they go to look at the thing we've discovered.

Their torches shine on the bin bag and Paolo clambers into the front of the car to block the view.

"I can't see," complains Lucas.

"That's the point," Paolo says. "I don't want you to see."

But we see enough.

Paolo calls Mum and the younger of the two policemen comes back to the car and talks to a disembodied voice over the radio.

I don't understand everything he says but I get the gist. It is a body...

He turns to face us.

"So what happened?" he asks.

Lucas points at me.

"It's his fault," I say, pointing back at him. "He dared me to open the box."

"What were you doing there? I mean, there's no path – or even a pavement."

"Walking home from school," says Lucas.

The policeman nods. His colleague is talking into a radio, and a moment later blue lights flicker around us. Another police car stops on the hill, and then a third. The other traffic stops.

"So what time was it?"

"An hour ago," says Lucas.

"Can I take them home?" says Paolo. "Actually, I'm on my bike, so can you take them home?"

The policeman ignores him. "Do you always come back this way?" he asks.

"Mostly, but in the car," I answer.

"Have you seen the box here before?" he asks.

"I think it was there on Friday evening, maybe Friday morning."

"Since Thursday morning," Lucas interrupts.

"Are you sure?" says Paolo.

"Yeah, I'm totally sure. That white mark there." He points at the tag on the box. "I first noticed it on Thursday morning."

The policeman drives us back but tells Paolo that we need to come to the police station tomorrow to make a statement.

Paolo rides in front and we leave the blue lights behind, weaving our way across the valley to the house. The policeman asks us about ourselves, in a not very interested way, and we reply in that automatic way that you reply to adults who aren't really listening.

I'm a block of ice, too cold even to shiver. Lucas can't stop shivering though, and the moment we get in the house he runs up the stairs to the bathroom. I sit on the kitchen radiator.

The policeman talks to Paolo in the hall. Sharing contact numbers, talking about trauma and shock, and I think about what I saw. What I felt. The shivers start as I'm sitting there. I need a hug; I need someone to hug me. This is too weird. Too shocking.

Kicking off my shoes and socks I head for the stairs when I hear a commotion and Mum crashes through the door, "Ruby! Ruby!" She bashes past the policeman and hurtles towards me, enveloping me in a massive warm, Mum-smelling embrace. "Are you all right? Do you feel all right? You're so cold!" She rubs my arms and hugs me and pulls a blanket off the sofa and wraps it around me and I don't answer because I can't.

"Hot drinks," she says, switching on the kettle. "And now tell me." She stands in front of me, expectant.

So I do, and it's short and, really, there's nothing she doesn't already know.

The policeman leaves and Lucas comes down, wrapped in towels and a dressing gown and still shivering.

He sits at the end of the table, staring into the distance like he's seeing things that aren't there.

I race upstairs, take a shower and then, rather

than texting Mia, run back down and sit at the table too. I understand now why Lucas has come down. I need to be around real, living people. Ones who don't ask millions of questions.

Mum and Paolo are being extra busy in the kitchen, while we sit in silence.

I begin to shiver again. Not from cold. I think it's shock. I think I'm in shock.

They're talking quietly. "Yes, it was a person," says Paolo.

"Do we know who?" asks Mum. "And what were the kids even doing there?"

"Walking home, apparently," says Paolo. "Although not the way I'd have gone."

"I'll never forgive myself. I was only answering the same old questions at the surgery. How stupid!"

"Not your fault," says Paolo, putting his arm around her shoulders. "And they didn't really see anything. I was there less than ten minutes after they telephoned me."

Lucas grabs an envelope. *We need to talk*, he scribbles on the back, before crossing it out so hard that the paper gives way.

We eat in silence. Finally Mum says, "So —

Hairspray. How's it going?"

"S'OK," says Lucas.

"Yeah," I agree.

Lucas looks across at me, his finger pointing up at the ceiling.

I widen my eyes.

Mum presses me. "Surely it must be fun? You love singing, Rube, don't you?"

"Yes, yes, I do," I say a little too brightly, and then I find myself wittering about the rehearsals without saying anything mean about Lucas. I don't mention people laughing, or the fact that he can't dance. Instead I say, "Lucas is really good at singing."

"Of course," says Paolo. "His great grandfather was a famous singer back in San Remo, a bass — chip off the old stone!"

"Block, darling," says Mum. "Chip off the old block."

I give up on food and push my plate away.

Next to me, Lucas does the same.

"Show us! I can play the piano part, I think," Paolo says.

"Not now, Pa. I reckon I just want to go up, if

that's OK."

Paolo looks disappointed.

"You two can watch a movie together," I say. "Night."

"It's him, isn't it?" says Lucas.

I nod.

We're sitting on the landing together, Paolo and Mum talking downstairs, the click of the central heating keeping us company.

"Why?" says Lucas.

"Exactly," I say.

In bed I text Mia, and she calls me straight away.

"It was on the news," she says. "I bet the telly people would really like to talk to you."

"There's no way that's going to happen." I shiver. "I don't want to think about it."

"But who was it?"

I hesitate. "I don't know..." I say.

"Is the doctor at your mum's still missing?"

"Yup," I say, closing the call and pulling the duvet up over my head.

Chapter 8

"Are you sure you can face school?" asks Mum. "I'm sure they'd understand."

"S'fine," I say. I reach into my pocket to see if my lunch card is there and find the thing I found on the side of the road yesterday. I take a look at it. It is indeed small and hard and seems to be a sizeable animal tooth with a gold lump on the end. The gold bit has a loop that's bent, like it broke off something. A necklace? A charm bracelet? An odd thing though.

"What's that?" says Mum, packing her lunch

into a box.

"Dunno. I found it yesterday."

"What? By the body?" She picks it out of my palm and washes the dirt off under the tap. "Yuk. A bit of bling. A dog's tooth? Has to be, too big to be anything else. Did you show the police?"

"It wasn't by the body. Further up the hill." I take it from her and put it back in my pocket. "I'll mention it to the police this afternoon when we give our statements."

Mum raises an eyebrow. "It's probably nothing," she says.

We drive the long way round. The hill's shut; no surprise there. And we make school just as the bell rings. Lucas waits until I get out of the car.

"Talk to you later," he mutters.

"Fine," I reply under my breath, and we head towards our separate tutor groups. I walk into mine and nobody looks up or gasps. Good, no one knows about yesterday. They've all heard about the body, but they don't know who found it and I hug Mia as I sit down beside her.

"Thank you," I say. "You kept it quiet."

"Course." She frowns at me. "You're my friend. I'll keep quiet as long as you need me to."

We go to rehearsal at lunchtime. The dance sequences work much better than yesterday and for half an hour I completely forget about the body on the hill, although Miss Johnson keeps looking at me like I lost both my parents in an air crash, so I'm guessing that everyone in the staff room knows. How long before the whole school knows?

"Now, Lucas, shall we have a go at your song?"

Lucas steps out and meets my eye. I give him an encouraging smile and he begins. It's all going really well for about three lines, and then he loses it. I don't know if he forgets the words, or the tune, but it goes patchy, then he stops altogether and finally Miss Johnson stops playing.

Trixie and Siobhan laugh. I mean properly, in a mean-girl snarky way, and I surprise myself by feeling indignant – hurt. Furious, even – all on Lucas's behalf.

I smile at him and try to catch his eye, but all he can do is look at his feet and the tips of his ears burn red.

We're saved from more by Miss Johnson pointing

at the clock.

"Time," she says.

Paolo agreed that we'd make our statements after
school. We drive to the police station without
speaking. He's helpfully loaded the *Hairspray*
soundtrack on to his phone so now we can listen
to it all the time. Lucas sits in the front, staring
out of the window. I sit in the back as we weave
through the traffic towards Bristol and a light snow
falls while Paolo sings along to the music. Before
long I'm doing the same, but I don't think Lucas
joins in. It's difficult to tell because Paolo is so
loud and exuberant that he completely drowns out
everything else.

The police station is underwhelming. Kind of
like school. Lucas and I go separately to make our
statements, each time with Paolo present.

"And is there anything else you can think of,
Ruby?"

I turn the tooth over in my pocket. I don't want
to bring it out and look stupid. On the other hand,
perhaps it's really important.

I put it on the table.

The police officer raises her eyebrows.

"That's a—" she starts.

"Where'd you find that?" asks Paolo.

"Up the hill – just on the verge bit. Do you think it's important?"

The police officer reaches for her iPad and brings up a map. "Could you mark where you found it on here?"

I expand the map and turn it to satellite. "There," I say pointing.

The woman scans up and down the road in street view. "Hmm," she says. "Quite a way off then. I don't think it's got anything to do with it."

I shrug. "S'pose not, but I thought you ought to see it."

"OK," she says. "I'll take a pic, but you can hang on to it for now. Did either of you discard the crisp packets that we saw in the lay-by…?"

We bundle back in the car and weave through stop-start traffic to the surgery. Mum comes out, locks the door behind her and climbs into the back seat next to me. She babbles about her day, offers a pack of Polos around the car and we start for home. There's this massive silence. After an age, Lucas asks, "Was it him?"

In the dark I can't really see her face but she sniffs. "Yes. It is. Was. Anna went to identify him. Poor thing. She's gone to stay with her sister now. No question it was murder. The police are taking their house apart."

"How awful," says Paolo.

"I know," says Mum. "I can't believe it."

"He's such a nice man." Paolo stops to let a woman pushing a buggy across the road. "Why would anyone kill him?"

We go down Brassknocker Hill and pass the lay-by. "Sorry," Paolo says as the car comes to a halt right next to where the box was.

Mum leans over and squeezes my hand. "How are you feeling today, love?" she whispers. I smile back. I don't need to answer. She knows.

All the way, tiny flakes of something icy fall from the sky. Sometimes they whizz towards the windscreen but all the time they catch in the headlights of the other cars. They're mesmerising.

"D'you think it's going to settle?" I ask.

"Hopefully," mumbles Lucas.

"Snow day, eh?" says Mum, and I think back to the last snow day. A few years back; I was at primary. Mum was dating Paolo but I don't think I knew what that meant except I suddenly had a babysitter who couldn't make me go to bed and didn't know that I was eating chocolate under the duvet. Or perhaps she did. The school didn't open and the whole village went sledging in the fields behind the shop. It was ace. I wonder what a snow day would be like with Lucas. Does he even know how to sledge?

We swing around the corner into the lane and Paolo pulls into our driveway. In the next-door garden is a tall tree hanging with warm white lights. From my bedroom it looks like an elephant. Paolo calls it the *"Natale"*. Mum says you can use it to navigate for miles. I don't think that's true, but it's welcoming.

Lucas is first out of the car and he runs for the front door. I follow him through the gate but he stops dead and I crash into his back.

"What the—"

"Oh!"

The front door is smashed in.

"Dad!" he calls.

"Mum!"

Paolo appears behind us. "Oh, hell," he says.

"I could so do without this," says Mum, pulling her mobile out of her pocket.

We probably shouldn't, but we go in anyway. I can hear Mum calling from below, but Lucas grabs a walking pole and I arm myself with a badminton racket and we stumble up the stairs. The landing looks OK but our bedroom doors are open and my shoes are spewed through the doorway. I stop, holding my badminton racket in front of me, Lucas alongside. He pushes his door open with the walking pole and leaps forward, flailing it above his head.

"Oh!" he says, and I follow him into his room. All the computers have gone. Instead, there are empty squares in the dust. His mattress is on its side. His bedside cabinet open and empty. Everywhere there are piles of stuff, books, socks, shoes, paper. The carpet's smothered and all the shelves are bare.

I turn, and with my heart in my shoes I push open my bedroom door. It's the same. Everything trashed. Everything on the floor. Empty shelves, cupboards, boxes. All my clothes dragged out from under my bed and scattered. My pretty little Victorian jewellery box that Granny gave me upside down and with the hinge broken. My duvet cover ripped off. Literally ripped. The stuffing from my pillow sprinkling everything. Sad snow.

I pick up a lone Lego figure that must have been under my bed and is now lying crushed under a trainer. It's a diver. I clutch it in my fist.

Lucas appears behind me. He says a string of words I can't repeat but that I agree with.

I can't say anything. I'm too shocked.

Paolo thunders up the stairs. "You'd better come down – the police want to see it for themselves. Come on."

The world is hyper real. I see everything in clear detail. The pile of DVDs at the top of the stairs, the dust on the picture frames. The bathmat hanging over the side of the bath. It's home, but it doesn't feel that way. At the bottom of the stairs we file out, back into the car, and sit and wait.

Chapter 9

We're at Granny's.

It's cramped but Mum says we're lucky we can stay with her, that there's nowhere free while the Christmas market's on and surely I don't mind staying in her old bedroom with her.

But I do, and I'm starting to feel quite angry. It's beginning to feel personal. And although part of me wants to run away, part of me is getting ready for a fight. It's been a hideous few hours, so I lock myself in the peach-coloured bathroom with matching towels and loo paper and run a peach foam bubble bath. It's very hot. I must be turning into a lobster, but I stay in and stare at the squares of ugly tiles on the wall and think back over the last few hours.

The police did come, eventually. We sat in the car until they arrived and they interviewed us there, in the dark. Mum and Paolo both went into the house to look at what was missing, then they let Lucas go in because they wanted to know about the computers, but they told me to stay put.

I'd asked if it was just burglars, and Mum had stared out of the window at the blue reflections bouncing off the white paint of our house. "What do you think?"

I watched as Lucas came back to the car. He was in tears. I know that computer means everything to him; he built it himself.

"Sorry about..." I began as he sat down next to me.

"It is what it is," he said. "Now I'll have more time to rehearse snotting *Hairspray*."

Then we drove to a restaurant in town and ate pizza surrounded by Christmas music, but it was all I could do to smile at the waitress.

Mum and Paolo talked about Dr Price and I chewed the pizza that felt like cardboard in my mouth. None of us ate all our food. Lucas kept his head down throughout and I remembered the state of my room.

"Cheer up," said Mum, poking me, but I didn't feel like cheering up. I felt victimised. Why was this happening to us?

It was like all the chit-chat was just covering the real thing underneath. The awfulness of Dr Price being murdered. Of us finding the body. Of us having our house trashed.

"Why?" I said when a sticky toffee pudding arrived in front of me.

"I thought you wanted it."

"No, why did anyone kill Dr Price? What did he know? What had he done?"

"Yeah, no, exactly," said Lucas. "This isn't random theft. It's targeted."

Mum and Paolo sat opposite staring at us as if we were stuffing the elephant in the room down their throats, which I suppose we kind of were.

And now I'm in the bath trying to understand what's been going on.

I leap out of the bath and, glowing like a lava lamp, I rub myself down and put on the pyjamas that Mum brought for me.

Our room is too hot. It's over the kitchen and I can hear the rumbling of voices downstairs.

Opening the window to cool down for a minute I watch a lone snowflake land on the tiles of the back porch. It lasts a second before it melts. I sit on Mum's saggy old bed and, looking out towards the swimming lake, wait for another. It's like waiting for shooting stars; they don't happen when you're concentrating. Snowflakes fall when you least expect them. I don't want a snow day. I want to go to school, to feel normal. I want to do rehearsals for *Hairspray* and get ready for Mia's party.

I close the window, put on a tartan dressing gown that must have been Mum's in the last millennium and pad downstairs. Donald is lying across the bottom and raises his head as I come down. He's been shut out of the kitchen and is probably sulking. He's certainly been farting.

"Sorry, old thing," I say, stepping over him.

Someone's tidied Granny's walking aids into a corner so I manage to get into the kitchen unannounced. The kitchen is large, and has a big table in the middle of it where Granny does almost everything. Her steam-age laptop is open at the end and Lucas is sitting behind it, swearing quietly to himself. Further along the table, Granny has got the Scrabble out and Paolo and Mum are dutifully rearranging plastic tiles. There are loads more spaces we could be in, but Granny doesn't use the front room unless she's watching TV, which she does at full volume while on her exercise bike. It's not very relaxing. Also, it's Donald's zone. There are four bedrooms upstairs, but one of them is full of boxes and another is full of Granny. And truthfully, it feels good being in the same space as everyone else.

I sit down at the end of the table next to Lucas. He looks terrible. His face is grey.

"OK?" I ask.

He nods.

But I know he isn't.

Shuffling closer, I peer round at the screen, expecting to see gaming or a maths site or something, but he's googling the murder on Brassknocker Hill. He doesn't turn the screen away from me, so I shuffle my chair round slightly so that I can see better. There are lots of results, some from national sites, most from local papers. He clicks on one and comes up with Dr Price. There's a picture of him and I remember his kind face beaming over a box of chocolates that he gave me when I was six or seven. It was lovely. A box of chocolates all to myself. Such a kind man. I can't believe he was that thing we found wrapped up in a bin liner.

The article Lucas's chosen doesn't say anything we don't know. No one is helping with inquiries and no one links the murder with the spate of break-ins.

"Useless," says Lucas.

"Hmm," I say. "So what do we know?"

He glances along to the Scrabble players who are sitting in tense, absorbed silence. Looking at the score sheet, Granny's winning. Not surprising; she always does.

"Just taking a load of bloatware off this computer and we can make a document. Share stuff, maybe?"

Sharing? That's something Lucas has never mentioned before. I watch as he deletes files from the hard drive. Fast and confident. This is obviously his happy place. I wouldn't have a clue.

While he's doing it, I type the things we know into my phone. I can copy and paste it all in a minute.

Dr Price is dead.

Dr Price went missing on Wednesday last week.

He was in a box on the hill by Thursday morning.

Jacqui, who works for him, had a break-in on Saturday morning.

We had a break-in today. (Nothing but computers missing, but our rooms super trashed.)

We were the ones who discovered the body.

An authorisation pings through from Lucas's gaming account letting me into a document.

I paste my facts; he pastes his.

They're basically the same.

Then he types:

So why would our bedrooms be more interesting to them than Sally and Paolo's?

And I type:

Because we found the body?

Lucas sits back and looks at me. "But what difference does that make? And who knows it was us?"

Paolo glances up. He sees me and Lucas sitting together and smiles. I know he'd like us to feel more like brother and sister, but we can't. We've both been only children and it's not that easy. Still, I'm trying to bond with my Step and it feels as if my Step is trying to bond with me.

Staring at Granny's collection of chipped china mugs from around the world I think through everything that happened when we found the body. The rubbish on the side of the lay-by? That was surely nothing to do with it. The slight snow, the cold.

Would it just have stayed there for months? I type.

Lucas shrugs. "Maybe."

Mum's phone rings and she stands up to talk out in the hall. It's Jacqui again.

"S'all feeling very ... up close," I murmur.

"For sure," he says.

I point upstairs. He raises his eyebrows and I leave the table, saying goodnight to Granny and Paolo on the way. They both hug me as if they'll never see me again, and for a moment I feel wobbly, but by the time I've stomped up the stairs and settled on to the ancient quilt that covers the put-up bed on the floor it's rage, not self-pity, that's reigning in my head.

A moment later Lucas taps on the door and comes in. He sits on Mum's bed under the window and I can't help but laugh. He's still wearing his school suit, all black, and he's sitting on this vile flowery quilt that must have been bought some time back in the chintz age from a department store that has rightfully closed. Mum's room has wallpaper too – disturbing combinations of peach and rose and lilac, and a tomato-soup carpet. Tinned, with added milk. I've always loved this room though, because it also has all Mum's rosettes from gymkhanas pinned to the wall, and funny photos of her on fat ponies that she must have really loved. It's also got pics of Grandpa, who was grumpy and smelled of tobacco but kind, very kind. I think Mum was a daddy's girl.

I'm not. I'm definitely my mum's.

Lucas overheats in a second and takes off his blazer. The sharp stink of teenage armpit leaks into the room. It's foul, but at least it's honest. I'd rather have that than cheap deodorant, but I suspect most of the girls at our school wouldn't.

"I could open the window?" I say.

"Oh, yeah," says Lucas, and he leans round to unfasten the catch.

This could be the first time we've been alone in a room together.

"So…" I begin.

"We need to know more," he says. "If this is a challenge we have to crack, then we need more information."

"Yeah, sure, but where from?"

"Your mum. Or Jacqui – or … Oskar, is it?"

"I don't think Mum really knows anything – but I agree there's some information out there that the killer wants to hide."

"How do you know that?" he asks.

"Well, because…" I think for a minute. "If Oskar's right, Dr Price knew something, or worked something out about someone. That someone didn't like it, and tried to destroy it, and him. But somewhere there's a loose end that's been left behind – or they wouldn't have needed to break into Jacqui's house or trash the surgery."

"I'd bet it's on the hard drives that were stolen from the surgery," he says. "I mean, do you buy that stuff about precious metals? Oskar was right about that. If you want gold, you take a catalytic converter, not a motherboard."

"Did they take all that stuff from your computer?"

"Dunno, they took the whole poxy thing." He kicks the bedside table, knocking a pink teddy off the top. He picks it up and places it carefully back where it was sitting.

We sit in silence for a minute.

"But they've got all that," says Lucas. "So there must be something else incriminating out there and we must have had access to it after they trashed the surgery."

"Something you might have had on your computer? Or that might have been in my bedroom inside my actual duvet?"

"Or that your mum brought back home and hid."

"But she didn't bring anything back."

"Yeah, but they don't know that. So they're going to go on looking if they think we have it."

"Does this make you really cross?" I ask.

"Furious," he replies.

"I'm fulminating. Incandescent, in fact. I'm so enraged!"

Lucas stares at me as if I'd grown a carrot out of the top of my head. "Yeah, me too," he says. "So we need to get to whatever it is before the killer does."

I giggle. "That's probably the most terrifying thing I've ever heard anyone say."

Chapter 10

Breakfast is madness. Granny is so loving having us all that she's stumbled down in total darkness and is trying to cook a traditional fry-up. Personally, I'm well up for it – I'm always hungry – but Mum insists on taking over and Granny's exciting notion of bacon, sausages and mushrooms is replaced by scrambled eggs on toast.

Mum drives us to school. In the queue of traffic on the way I ask her if there is anything else she can remember about Dr Price. Any other details about him before he disappeared.

"Poor man, I can't think of anything useful. It's just a blur, really."

"Did he carry a briefcase?" asks Lucas.

Mum shakes her head. "Not really, he always travelled light, usually on foot, or sometimes on his electric bike."

"Where did he keep the bike when he was at work?" I ask. "I'm sure I've never seen it at the surgery."

"He rented a lock-up nearby, kept a few other bits and pieces there too. Actually, thinking about it, I don't know who else knows about it, though I suppose his wife must. I managed to get it for him at a very low rent from Mrs Parks when her husband died and she said she just wanted someone to use it."

"Where is it?" asks Lucas.

"Quarry Close," says Mum. "Just down the hill on the right."

We pull into school and Lucas taps me on the arm. "Quarry Close, see you later," he says, vanishing into C Block.

School feels so weird. I sit next to Mia at tutor and

her eyebrows practically join her scalp when I tell her about the break-in.

I promise I'll tell her everything in art.

Unfortunately, in art we have a supply teacher who splits us up and makes us all stay in our seats. I don't really blame him because Zak spills red paint all over his hands and wanders around howling and quoting chunks from *Macbeth*.

Finally in the queue at break we get to speak. "They broke into your house?" she says.

I nod. "It feels like there's a loose end, something left over that the killer's looking for. Something he might think Mum has taken home with her."

"And was there anything?"

"Well, no. But there's this." I show Mia the tooth. "We found it near the body," I say. "Ish. Up the hill, really."

"Gold, eh?" she says. "And what's that embedded in it? Bone?"

"Tooth," I say. "Or at least that's what Mum said it was."

Mia wrinkles up her face in disgust. "Why would anyone have a tooth hanging off their neck, unless it's some kind of a gross hunting trophy. I bet the police were really interested though."

"Not really. Apparently it was too far away to have anything to do with the body. They were more interested in a skanky old crisp packet someone had dropped."

We grab paninis and cold chips and I wonder where they buy their mozzarella from because it definitely isn't where Paolo buys his. With the tepid chunks of white rubber going round and round on my tongue we make it into the rehearsal only a little late.

"Ah! Ruby! Mia! So pleased you could make it," says Miss Johnson. I don't think she's being sarcastic.

Before we get to sit down, Miss Johnson has us dancing. It's not too bad. Then we try it with Lucas centre stage. I'm willing him to succeed. I'm willing him to forget his fears and just dance. It's not terrible, but it's not good. I've never before seen a person wringing their hands but Miss Johnson does it as Lucas struggles through, swaying and bumping into everyone. Stumbling off the side and back on. Trixie is openly laughing again, so is Siobhan and so is Euan Henderson.

The anger that I've had building since last night boils over.

"Stop it, you lot. Just stop it!"

Miss Johnson swings round to face me. "What?"

"They're being mean – horrible. Look at them!"

Miss Johnson switches off the tape. "Are they? What?"

"Just now, they were laughing, sniggering. At Lucas."

Trixie shoots me a look of death but I don't care.

"It's not his fault. He's just not…" I look at Lucas. He too is giving me a death look.

"Just not what?" asks Miss Johnson.

"Nothing," I say.

I got that one wrong.

The rest of the day is unbearable. Trixie tries to trip me as I go to PSHE. I manage not to make a fool of myself. Siobhan makes a fuss about where to sit in music. She's supposed to sit next to me. We do half an hour's frozen hockey out on a frozen pitch where both of them go full nasty. I'm lucky to escape with my ankles intact.

After hockey, Mia and I have food tech.

"She's such a cow," says Mia.

"Isn't she?" I say. I stir the gloop that's supposed to be a cheese sauce. I'm not really thinking about Trixie, I'm thinking about Lucas.

"Should have kept my mouth shut," I say.

"It's like poking a hornet's nest," she says. "Once you've set her off..."

"I shouldn't have tried to support Lucas. I read that all wrong. He'd rather have gone down in flames than have me stick up for him."

"Why?"

"I dunno, but maybe he felt it was patronising. You know – like he can't stick up for himself or something." I sigh. "It's just that finding the body together – it was sort of bonding, and I'm trying hard to get closer to him. But..."

"You're solving a mystery together, that's very bonding." Mia squeezes my arm and changes the subject. "Listen, do you think I should order pizza for my birthday or make a load of canapé things – you know, go classy? Or maybe we could go skating? Actually, we could go and take a look at the rink in town after school?"

* * *

But at half past three, we're surprised by Lucas. He's waiting for me. For a second I think he's going to lay into me for trying to stand up for him, but he says, "Quarry Close?"

He glances from me to Mia and back and widens his eyes theatrically.

Mia glances from me to Lucas and back. "Tell you what, I'll go and see the skating rink on my own. You guys can 'Quarry Close', whatever that is."

"Mia?" I say as she sets off out of the car park.

"S'cool," she turns and calls back to us. "You need to find out what's going on. Tell me tomorrow, OK?"

"Is this like, OK?" says Lucas. "I didn't mean to, you know, butt in."

"I think it's fine," I say. And it is fine, isn't it? It's just the first time, ever, I've chosen to do something with my Step and not my friend.

In silence we set off along the main road to Quarry Close.

It's dark, more or less, and within a few minutes my phone tells me to go left and we leave the main pavement and take a bumpy tarmac road that runs along the back of some houses.

"It's here somewhere," I say, zooming in on my phone screen.

"I reckon it's at the end – yes, look, there are some garages." Lucas strides ahead and I follow into a dark cul de sac, passing through a line of trees and skirting piles of building rubble. On my phone I can see it's a circular quarry, but standing here it's just a wasteland.

"I can't hear the traffic," I say.

Lucas pauses. Listening. There's a wash of orange sunset behind the trees, but everything in front of us is shades of dim. A long block of six garages and a pad of concrete sit in the middle of the space. On either side is masonry and bramble. There are no lights. No people.

"How do we know which one it is?" he asks, his voice quieter than normal.

"Process of elimination," I say, approaching the left-hand end of the block. Not far away something rustles in the bushes. Hairs rise on the back of my neck.

"Try the doors," I say.

I push the first one. It slides up and I squint

into the gloom. A cold cavernous empty space. "Nothing here," I say.

"OK," says Lucas, pushing the one next to me and jumping back when the door clangs open.

Inside is a locked car.

Another is open with nothing inside.

The fifth is unlocked and jammed with chairs.

Which leaves the sixth.

"How do we know it wasn't one of those ones that opened?" whispers Lucas.

"It should have his electric bike in it," I say.

"Well, this one's locked." Lucas sighs. "We can't—" There's the sound of stone on stone, very nearby. "What was that?"

"I dunno," I say, frantically running my fingers along the sill at the bottom of the door and down the sides of the locked garage in case there's a key.

Lucas has his back to the garage and is shining his torch into the bushes. "There's something out there."

"Hang on," I say, patting the sides of the building.

"Hurry up," whispers Lucas.

"Ah!" I say, my thumb catching on a nail sticking out of the back wall. There's a tinkling sound as something patters against the concrete. "Yessss!"

Lucas swings his torch back to the door and we struggle to unlock it with our frozen fingers. The key turns and we pause. "Ready?" I ask.

Lucas answers by bending down and lifting the bottom of the door until it's fully open.

The bike stands in the middle, flanked on either side by neatly labelled boxes. I flick my torch on and run the light over the cardboard. "China, books, linen."

"Videos and DVDs here," he says. "Are we going to go through them all?" he asks, opening and closing the flaps on a box marked *CDs Classical.* "There's so much."

"No," I say. "I'm disappointed. I thought there'd be something more obvious."

"Hey," says Lucas. "What's this?" He holds up a brown envelope.

"Where'd you find that?"

"Bike basket," he says.

"Let's—"

"Terrible shame," says a voice behind us.

I jump. Lucas swings his torch round. Behind us is a white-haired man wearing a scarf over half his face and a coat pulled close at the collar. He doesn't look cross, just sad. "A shame about Dr Price – such a lovely man."

"Yes," I say. "He is – was. My mum worked for him. Miss Parker."

"At the surgery?" asks the man.

Next to me Lucas is nodding furiously. "Yes, that's right," he says.

I paste a smile on my face and try to look relaxed. This must seem very odd. Two teenagers breaking into a lock-up in the dark. I pull the smile tighter. Maybe I'm trying too hard, so I let it drop a little. But the man doesn't seem worried by us. "And to think he was only here a few days ago – putting his bike away on Wednesday morning. We had a nice chat."

"Oh?"

"Yes. He was worried about something in that envelope you've stuffed under your jacket."

"What, this?" says Lucas with an uncomfortable cough.

"I was wondering whether to tell the police about it – but if your mum works at the surgery, you can do that. Take care then," he says, whistling to an invisible dog and strolling off into the darkness. "And watch your step."

With demons at our backs we run from the garage towards the main road.

"I can't believe we did that," I say, sucking in lungsful of fumes from the line of traffic jammed at the roundabout.

"Nor can I," Lucas giggles. "And that bloke turning up in the dark – freaky!" He pulls an inhaler out of his pocket and takes two giant breaths. "That's better. Bus? Home?"

We walk back to school, but the last bus has gone.

"Town then," says Lucas. "Race you."

We half run, half walk down the hill. I'm desperate to look inside the envelope, but it's windy and sleeting and now is not the time or place.

We turn into Bathwick Street and I get a text from Mum.

Are you in town? I'm still at the surgery. Give you a lift if you walk up?

"We've just come from there," says Lucas. "Seriously?"

"We can walk through the Christmas market," I say. "Come on. We'll be up there in twenty minutes. And honestly, the buses are rammed this time of year. We might not even get on. Be much nicer getting a lift."

"Oh, OK," he mutters, and we plunge into the crowds.

There are thousands of people milling around and the air smells spicy and delicious. This morning Granny wouldn't let me go to school without a coat and for once I'm grateful. I push my hands deep into my pockets and wander into the crowds around the market stalls. I've got my bank card with me, so I could buy Mum a present. I stop to look at soaps made in Glastonbury, but they all smell weird and are full of things like patchouli and neroli, whatever that is.

Mum's fussy; she likes stuff she can recognise.

"Are we shopping or going home?" mutters Lucas.

Making a mumbled excuse to the stall-keeper, I step backward and blunder straight into someone who was standing very close behind me. It's a man who is all scarf and hat, and he turns away, vanishing into the crowd. We plunge on through the market, heading roughly for the surgery although I'm looking out for something that Mum would like. I'm not finding anything, and I get a sudden sense of someone tugging on my pocket. I swing round but it's just a sea of coats and hats and scarves. I apologise to no one and, grabbing Lucas's sleeve, take off towards the Guildhall market where the crowds are thinner.

"What the...?" he asks.

I stop there, my back to the wall, and look at the people. "We're being followed."

We stand next to each other, staring out into the milling mass of people.

"No one's looking at us."

"Just now, someone had their hand in my pocket."

"Oh," he says.

"Have you still got the envelope?"

"Yup," he says. "It's digging into my armpit."

We dive sideways towards the Guildhall market, barging through the crowds, and then swing back round to emerge on the street opposite the Society Café. As I glance back down the alleyway into the heart of the market a shadow slips to the side.

Although we ultimately want to go the other way, we head up town passing Waitrose on our right, where a thousand people a second are pouring in and out of the doors, then swing left into New Bond Street where the Christmas decorations that look like suspender belts are out showing their bling for the hundredth year running. Ducking into the entrance of Green Street I check that no one's following us, although I really can't tell. There are so many people swarming, dragging kids and shopping and mostly looking a little desperate.

Agreeing to meet back by the station, we split in Milsom Street. Lucas goes for Jolly's while I dart into Waterstones, up the stairs to the cookery books, pretend to check them out and then go straight down in the lift. I double back towards the kids' department, where there's a woman in pink glasses rearranging the Peppa Pig display. "Can I help?" she asks, but I flee, striding towards the front of the shop where there's a big queue. Perfect. I'll burrow through and then out the other side. With only a little swearing, I make it to a different set of doors and dive into the stream of people heading down Milsom Street.

I stay in the mass until I reach the carousel outside the Pump Rooms and take the stall-filled back alley that brings me into the abbey courtyard. Leaving the market again, I jog down the side of the Huntsman pub and leg it towards the station. Hordes of people are heading for the trains so it's easy to stay with them until the last second, when I nip under the railway line and come out in the car park at the back.

Lucas is there already, breathing hard. He's holding a paper bag.

"Went out the back of Jolly's and looped through Mr B's bookshop just to be safe. Bought a book for Dad."

He can't see me raise my eyebrows, but I do. Shopping, while being pursued? Nerves of steel.

There's a steady flow of people right through to Widcombe so we mingle with them and run across the road when the crossing man is still showing red.

A shudder runs down my back and I break into a jog.

Alongside me, Lucas speeds up too. The crowds are thinner here; we'd be easier to spot.

Skirting the main parade of shops we sprint up the hill, past tall houses with their shutters pulled close but the warm lights of Christmas showing through the gaps. I'm warm. Actually I'm boiling in this coat but I daren't slow down, and after a couple more roads we get to the surgery. The main light outside is off, but I can see the lights on inside.

I bash on the door. "Mum! It's us!"

Clanking and rattling, she opens up, leaving us to close the door behind ourselves.

Lucas goes on into the surgery while I lean against the door checking the latch is down and sucking in huge lungfuls of air. My heart's going bonkers. Running or fear? I'm not sure. Glancing up I look out through the little square of glass in the door. A figure breaks from the shadows opposite and walks up the hill. Tall. Black coat, black hat.

Am I just being paranoid?

Chapter 11

I take my coat off and go through into the lobby
to join Lucas.

It's the first time I've been here since the break-in
and I can smell the burned plastic from the fire.

The waiting room looks fairly normal but when
I enter the office I can see the damage.

"What the—"

"Do you want a cup of tea?" asks Mum.

"Oh, are we not going home straight away?"

"Bit of a panic," she replies. "Oskar didn't come
in today. I'm trying to make sense of his stock check

system, which I really must do before tomorrow or we'll be all over the place."

Lucas raises an eyebrow. "We could…" He pulls the corner of the letter from the inside of his jacket.

"Sally!" says Jacqui, emerging from the back office, waving a piece of paper. "Look – look what I've found." One glance and she's clocked us. "Lucas, Ruby! Hello."

She puts the paper on the desk, sweeping aside a pile of other documents and standing back, tutting. "It's the bank statement, for here, for the practice. Look," she says, pointing. "Every week you can see the wages going out – there, see, and the income coming in – there."

Lucas and I lean forward to look. Two columns. In and out.

"But what's that?" I say, pointing at £450 that's not got a name next to it.

"Exactly," says Jacqui. "That's cash. A cash withdrawal."

"Why would the practice need £450 in cash? We only buy tea and coffee," says Mum.

There's a long silence while Mum stares at the

bank statements and Jacqui stares at Mum staring at the bank statements.

"You're saying someone's been taking cash out of the business?" says Lucas.

"Several times," says Jacqui, holding up a handful of printouts.

"Embezzlement," says Mum. "But how did Dr Price not see this?"

Jacqui tilts her head. "Perhaps he did."

"Who has access to the bank accounts?" I ask.

"All of us," says Mum. "Basically any of the administrators can withdraw money – but surely the bank would have asked questions? Wouldn't they ring the surgery?"

"Not for such small amounts," says Jacqui. "If you look, it's £300 here, £250 there. The biggest one is £500. But it adds up."

"To what?" I say. "How much in total?"

"I don't actually know," says Jacqui. "Ten thousand, maybe twice that."

"Oh, lordy," says Mum. "This is awful."

"Whose job is it to check the bank statements?" asks Lucas, counting something on his fingers.

"Well, mine – and Oskar's. He's done it for the

last few months," says Jacqui. "He insisted and I was grateful because I'm no good at numbers. No good at all."

Mum stands back and I look through Jacqui's printouts. They only go back six months and I can see that the amounts vary a lot. "It's an average of about £450 a week, week after week."

"Why did no one notice?"

"Perhaps Dr Price did. It has to be Oskar."

"Really?" I say.

"Well, it wasn't me, and I don't think it was Dr Price. I think we should ring the police. Oskar's such a lovely boy. Who'd have thought it?"

We drink tea until the police come. I'm dying to look in the envelope but when I point at it, Lucas frowns and pulls his jacket closer.

I sit, impatient to get home.

It's the same pair again. Detective Sergeant Afolabi and Detective Sergeant Green. The man walks around looking at the pictures on the walls. I wonder what he learns? DS Afolabi looks even more tired than last time

"How's your daughter doing?" Jacqui asks straight

away. "Any better at sleeping? My Anthony was a nightmare."

DS Afolabi rubs her face. "Oh, it's exhausting. Three times in the night and then she cries her little heart out when I leave her at nursery."

"She's knackered," says the other police officer. "Lives on coffee."

"D'you want one now?" I ask.

DS Afolabi smiles for the first time since I first met her. "It's all right, sweetheart, I'm fifty per cent caffeine as it is. Now – tell me."

Mum explains it very clearly, with occasional interruptions from Jacqui. "So Oskar."

"Lovely Oskar," says Jacqui, playing nervously with a gold chain around her neck.

"He does the bank statements, handles the petty cash. He's kind of the practice manager, although part-time. Three days a week. He was due in today though."

"With me," says Jacqui. "Although I do loads of reception duty too, and he's more behind the scenes."

"Anyway, we haven't seen him since, what, Sunday?" Mum looks to Jacqui for help.

Jacqui nods.

"But look, there's all this money taken out of the practice bank account – and if you look in the safe there's only forty-two pounds sixty. So where's it gone?"

DS Afolabi looks up. "You think it's a motive?" she says.

"It adds up to twelve thousand three hundred and twenty pounds, just on those statements there." Lucas points.

"It could have been going on for longer." Jacqui sits on the desk.

"Can I take these?" says DS Afolabi.

"Sure," says Mum.

"We'll talk to the bank, see if we can get CCTV of the withdrawals, although the last one was—"

"Six weeks ago," says Jacqui.

The male police officer sits down for the first time. "Where does Oskar live? I think we should pay him a call."

Chapter 12

As we drive home I stare out at the passing cars.

"I'm in shock," says Mum. "Oskar. I mean, he's such a lovely lad. It's so unlikely."

I'm with her. The news is massive. Oskar's so kind. And he doesn't have a really flash lifestyle; no car, or partner to please.

I think it all through. Something strikes me. "If Oskar was found stealing from the surgery by Dr Price, and killed the doctor because he was too scared of being discovered or whatever — how, when he doesn't drive, did he dump the body on the hill?"

Mum nods.

"And if he doesn't drive," says Lucas, "how did he get out to our house and trash it?"

"He must have a friend — an accomplice."

"Hmm," I say. "It doesn't really explain the break-ins, does it?"

"No, it doesn't," says Lucas.

"I don't know," says Mum, sighing, "I'm just glad it's all over. It looks like we know what happened, and why. And he's vanished — run away. We'll just have to wait for the police to catch up with him. We can snuggle down and get on with Christmas now."

"Really?"

"Oh, yes, I think so. Don't you?"

When we reach the house Paolo has cleaned up and there's a smell of baking bread that reminds me I'm starving.

Lucas points upstairs and we both race up. "Be two minutes," I say, running into my room and checking how it looks. All tidy. Different, but not like it's just been burgled.

Paolo is amazing.

I throw off my uniform and change into PJs.

Lucas has left his door open and he's sitting behind his empty desk looking at his phone, where his computer ought to be.

"Oskar doesn't fit at all," he says. "Here, look."

He passes me the brown envelope, now pretty crumpled, and a piece of A4 paper.

It's a letter addressed to Dr Price.

From a pathology department in Nottingham.

It's full of scientific terms and numbers and it makes no sense to me at all. "What does it mean?"

"It's a toxicology report. I had to google most of it. It's the results of a test for various chemicals, acetone, methanol and poisons."

"Oh?"

"For this person, Rebecca Duncan Smith, who died, like, months ago, as far as I can make out. But see here — it says that there was a huge amount of morphine in her bloodstream. I've googled the quantity and that's, like, tons. And traces of arsenic in her hair."

I stare at the figures. I'm glad I've got Lucas here — it would mean nothing to me. "Poison? So Dr

Price was asking if someone had been poisoned?"

"Looks like it," says Lucas, tapping his fingers on his desk.

"What's this written here?" On the back of the paper is an inky scrawl.

"I don't know. I was hoping you could read it."

"P – rem ... eth?"

"Now you say it out loud, could it read premature death?"

I hold the paper up to the light so that I can see the scrawl more clearly. "Yes, it could."

I sit back, fold the letter and slide it back in the envelope. "Someone was murdered. Dr Price found out. Then he was murdered. We should show the police."

"Yeah, although we broke into his garage to get it."

I stare at the wall. "My head feels very full."

"Mine too," says Lucas.

"Crisps," I say. "I need crisps. But, Lucas, bring it with you to school. We'll go to the police straight afterwards – yeah? Even if they tell us off for breaking in?"

He nods. "OK – you're right."

"Someone followed us. They must have been at the garage. The sooner we hand it over, the better. We don't have to tell Mum and Paolo that we broke in – just the police."

"They can find out who this woman was."

"Exactly. They can deal with the whole thing."

"Do you have an envelope? You know, disguise."

I find a green envelope covered in butterfly stickers that Mia put my birthday card in. It's got Ruby written on the front and it's smaller than the original.

Lucas folds the letter and puts it inside, before dropping it in his backpack.

We go down to eat veggie hot pot with dough sticks and we all slob in front of the TV to watch *Elf* for the millionth time.

In spite of the movie, and the sofa, and my family, a shudder runs down my back and I pull my dressing gown tight around my neck to stop it.

I know Mum and the police think it's all over. But it isn't. There's still someone out there.

I go to school the next day feeling uneasy. And I know I'm going to stay that way until that letter's with the police.

Halfway through the day, Mum sends a text saying *Case Closed except for finding Oskar* and I click my screen off. I try to remember exactly what the man in the market was wearing. A dark coat. A dark long coat. A bobble hat.

When we tell the police, they can check the CCTV. Just in case it's Oskar.

But it wasn't Oskar.

Another *Hairspray* rehearsal. Lucas sits next to Desta and they put their books on the same chair. She smiles at him as their books touch and he blushes and knocks the whole lot on the floor. I look away, reaching for my headphones so that I can't hear the laughter. As I search for them in my pocket my fingers brush the tooth ornament. Sitting in the corner of the drama studio, in the almost dark, I examine it again.

It's too big to be a human tooth. I turn it around to catch the light. And it's quite a big lump of gold. I'm still staring at it when Lucas thumps into the chair next to me and sits down.

I pull one earbud out of my ear.

"Thanks," he says. "For staying out of it."

"Whatever," I say.

"What's that?" he says, pointing into my palm.

I hand it over to him. "Remember?" I say. "I picked it up just before we found the body."

He nods. Turning his phone torch on and looking closer.

"I reckon," he says, "that belongs to a big cat."

"What, like a tiger? Some blingy tourist must've dropped it," I say, sitting back to enjoy Desta's singing again, but remembering just how close to the body I'd found the tooth. "Or do you think they were wrong at the police station and it *is* somehow connected to all this?"

Lucas stares at Desta. I think I see love in his eyes. Of course! *That's* why he's doing the show. Not sure how he thinks being bad at dancing is going to win her over though. She's very alpha.

"Sorry?" he says.

"Do you think this was dropped by the murderer? Do you think that's the thing they were looking for in our rooms?"

He stares at me for a moment.

"How would they know we'd found it?"

"Well, it's not at the murder scene any more."

"But the police might have discovered it," he says. "So who knows *we* found it?"

"The police. Mum. Paolo. Anyone who knows us. That does include Oskar."

"But it isn't Oskar, is it?" he asks. "I mean, he doesn't drive and he wasn't the one following us last night. And you don't think he's a murderer."

I watch the stage. Desta and the record-shop dancers, including Mia, are working through their act. They're much better than they were last week. Must have been rehearsing.

"No, but people never believe their friends are murderers, do they? I mean, Desta might be a murderer, but you wouldn't know it."

Lucas makes an awkward choking sound. I laugh quietly to myself. Gotcha! Maybe this brother-sister thing is easier than I thought.

"We'll take that and the letter to the police, yeah? Straight after school," he says.

I nod but he doesn't see me. His eyes are on Desta.

We meet on the bus into town. I'm primed to tell the truth to the police. I've rehearsed it with Mia.

All they can do is tell us off, but when I sit down next to Lucas, he's frantically going through his bag.

"It's gone," he says.

"The letter? How?" I ask. "At school?"

"Or at home, I suppose. But I'm sure I had it with me this morning."

"I saw you put it in your backpack last night. It must be there."

When the bus pulls into the bus station we go to the café at the back. I buy a cup of tea in a burn-your-fingers plastic cup and Lucas empties his bag. We look inside every book, shake every piece of paper and then do it all over again.

"It's not there," he says. And we check everything all over again but we can't find it.

Chapter 13

When we get home, Lucas tears his room apart. I sit on the landing and listen, but the letter has vanished.

"How could they have got hold of it?"

"Did you leave your bag anywhere at school?"

"Only during PE."

We sit in silence. In my mind I'm imagining which of the two thousand people who have access to the school could be a murderer.

"Darlings!" Mum calls up the stairs. "Can we talk about the wedding – clothes, hair, timings?"

Lucas lets out a long sigh and I go down to sit at the table and listen to Mum talking about nail varnish. It kind of stays like that for the next few days.

Mum gets into a pre-wedding spin. The murder is hardly mentioned, the police stop visiting us, and Mum and Jacqui seem content that Oskar, a person they've worked alongside for months, is a murderer. Or at least an embezzler.

Lucas and I, on the other hand, stay on high alert, asking everyone at school about the envelope, searching the house, googling Rebecca Duncan Smith, and getting nowhere.

In the end, we try to trace Oskar.

At the next rehearsal, we tell Mia about the letter and she suggests that we walk to Oskar's house after school and bang on the door. We wait impatiently as she finishes her dance. There's no Desta today. She's been off sick all week and Lucas is far less interested in the play than he was last week.

Finally, we leave the school in twilight. This time it's three teenagers standing in the gloom looking suspicious. The woman from the house next door to Oskar's sticks her head out to stare at us.

"Have you seen Oskar?" I ask, hoping it makes us seem a whole lot less dodgy.

She shakes her head. "No, not for days." We still knock on the door, but it's no surprise when he doesn't answer, and although I'm prepared to break into a garage, I'm not prepared to break into a house.

"Perhaps he did do the embezzling, but not the murdering, and he's gone on a cruise or something?"

That's as far as we get before the wedding panic takes over and that's mostly to do with clothes. Lucas is going to have to wear a suit, and from the expression on his face it's obviously a form of torture, and after she's bought me a new skirt to wear, Mum makes me have a haircut. The woman who trims it is really kind and she does these long cool curls and makes it all sleek and it seems a shame to sleep on it really.

We visit Granny to show her our outfits and I take the opportunity to hide the tooth in Mum's flowery bedroom. It really does seem the safest place.

On the day of the wedding it starts to snow and Jacqui rings to say that her son Anthony is doing a shuttle to and from the house if we don't want to drive. Paolo scoffs and says that in Italy he's used to driving on the snow but Mum points out that he has snow tyres there and there aren't any stupid English drivers on the road who don't know what they're doing.

Still, as Lucas says, the snow would barely fill an egg cup. Paolo collects Granny, who is wearing a rather lovely cherry velvet jacket that she says she bought in the 1960s. She looks incredibly cool. She puts Mum in a total tizz by making her go and change her outfit, all the while sitting on the sofa and eating biscuits.

"I need to get there early," says Mum. "I said I would."

The tension rises until we're ready to go and we all pile in the car. It's eleven thirty. Mia will be sitting down in Maths. I should be there too, but – weddings.

"Is Jacqui going to go on working at the surgery?" asks Granny as we head down the main road, snow slinging itself at the windscreen in white zigzag lines.

"Going to move to the Frome one," says Mum.

"Ah," says Granny. "You'll miss her."

"I will," says Mum, staring out of the window.

We reach the main gates of Darkwood House. "Never been through these," says Paolo. Darkwood is a safari park, and there are lots of signs to another set of gates for the visitors. This is the private entrance, hidden in the trees with an imposing pair of iron gates topped with snow-dusted lions.

"Impressive, isn't it?" says Mum. She jumps out, presses a button and talks to a disembodied voice. The gates swing wide and we trundle along the drive.

"Very nice," says Granny, wedged between me and the window.

The drive seems to go on forever but then we break over a hill and framed between two groups of trees stands the house. I've been before, of course I have, but never in the snow. It's so beautiful.

"Wow!" breathes Mum. She's right. It's totally picture postcard, the tall house, lights in every window, welcoming us in from the snow. Although there are one or two things in the landscape that aren't quite picture postcard: a herd of ostriches and a couple of wildebeest.

In the distance a figure in a high-vis jacket slightly spoils the effect of Victorian Christmas, but we head towards him and he points us to another pair of gates. "We're getting to go into the inner sanctum," says Granny. We drive over a cattle grid into a modest car park – only big enough for a hundred cars or so.

As Mum gets out, Paolo springs from the driver's seat, whips open an umbrella and holds the door for Granny. Lucas lets out a long sigh.

"I suppose we go in there?" says Granny, marching towards a door up a couple of steps. Paolo runs alongside and we follow. The door is miraculously opened by a man dressed in a tailcoat. "Seams on those trousers would spread butter," mutters Granny before stepping inside.

"Wow!" says Paolo. "This is..."

The room in front of us is massive. The walls, floor and ceiling are all made of wood – carved, polished, studded with deers' heads and antlers, coats of arms, swords and oil paintings. There are three fireplaces, each with a roaring fire. Vast glittering chandeliers hang from the ceiling, dancing the firelight around the walls. On the football-pitch-sized Persian rug, eight tables are laid with shining glasses and polished cutlery; in the centre of each there's an extravagant silvery flower arrangement dotted with robins and holly berries. In the corner furthest away from the fireplaces stands the tallest Christmas tree I've ever seen indoors. The golden star on the top is brushing the roof panels, and underneath there's a shedload of wrapped parcels, casually arranged like they're ready for a photoshoot.

We stand and stare.

"This way, please," says the tailcoat man, leading us out of the giant space into another smaller room, this one rammed with dainty chairs. A couple of women in sensible suits are discussing something behind a long table.

"Registrars," hisses Granny.

But we pass on through into a hall with a huge panelled staircase dotted with dark portraits of dismal-looking people wearing long-ago clothes. From there into a massive living room, with leather sofas, more fires and an alarming head on the walls, this time a tiger's flanked by a pair of giraffes'.

We sit down under a dead-eyed zebra and the

man offers us coffee and hot chocolate. We're so early there are only a few other people here.

"Well," says Granny. "This is very pleasant. Gosh, look at that." She points at a leopard's skin rug on the floor. "Once got the offer to go on safari, you know."

"Did you?" asks Paolo.

"Didn't. You know, as you get older it's the things you don't do that you start to regret." She sighs and takes a long slurp on her coffee. "Should have taken more risks in my life."

"Do you think I can wander around a bit?" I ask, dying to stand by the window and watch the snowflakes fall.

"Stay in this room," says Mum. "Although I could do with the loo."

Lucas joins me and we walk to the enormous windows that look out on to the park. The snow goes from scanty to blizzard and back again. The trees close by start to collect snow on their branches, but the far-away ones just turn a little greyer. A pair of yellow headlights appears to the left, followed by another. "Guests," I say. Lucas doesn't say anything.

I don't want to stare at him, but he actually looks quite good in the suit. It's one of Paolo's, probably Italian, and I realise that Lucas is almost as tall as his dad. If he'd raise his head and stop looking at the ground.

Behind us, the tailcoat man arrives with a huge tray and Granny makes happy noises as she finds biscuits and a "perfectly hot" cup of coffee.

Mum is swept away to do maid-of-honour duties and now the only sound is the crackling of the fire.

"Goodness," says Granny into the vacuum. The silence is yawning.

Lucas picks up a book from a small bookcase by the window. *Jane Eyre*. It's leather bound with fancy gold writing on the spine. He opens it and makes a strange choking sound before nudging me with his elbow. He holds the book out under my nose and I look down at it.

"*Jane Eyre*, edited by Currer Bell…"

"No — look here," he hisses, jabbing the page. "There."

Someone has written their name in careful handwriting. "Becca Smith," I say. "Becca Smith? Short for Rebecca?"

Lucas raises his eyebrows and closes the book. He picks out another: *The Mill on the Floss*. As the cover falls open I see the same careful script. The same name. He puts it back on the shelf and we stare fixedly out of the window, while behind us a door opens and another group of people are ushered in. Rebecca Smith. Rebecca Duncan Smith. I think back to everything I know about Jacqui's about-to-be-husband, Sebastian. Sebastian Duncan.

He's a widower, for one thing. His wife died two years ago. One year ago? What else do I know?

Dr Radcliffe, Dr Price's wife, arrives propped up by their daughter and Granny gets to her feet and goes over to make sympathy noises. Lucas is typing things into his phone. I angle myself to see his screen but Paolo wanders over to join us and sits on the window seat watching the snow.

"*Perfetto*," he mutters.

I hear a door open and close, and Mum scuttles back in. She's got a huge smile on her face. She'd think it weird if I wasn't interested in the wedding.

"And?" I say.

"Well." She leans forward. "The. Dress. Is. A – Mazing."

"What colour?" I ask.

"You'll see in a minute. Now, I think we should go through."

Making polite conversation as she goes, Mum makes her way through to the room cluttered with all the small chairs.

The man in the tailcoat throws the doors open and there's a steady trail into the room. Lucas and I hang back. Everyone there is over forty, maybe even over fifty, in fact. Mum's one of the youngest.

"Have you found anything?" I ask. Lucas keeps on pulling at his shirt. He does look massively uncomfortable.

"It's got to have been his wife. Becca Smith becomes Rebecca Smith, marries Sebastian and becomes Rebecca Duncan Smith. She died—"

Granny grabs both our hands. "Come on, dears, let's get a decent seat. I'm looking forward to the food."

The front row is empty, apart from Mum, so we dutifully file in and sit by her. I can feel eighty pairs of eyes staring at the back of my head and I keep my own fixed ahead on the two registrars. They're looking expectantly at the door at the back and there's a murmur as it opens, followed by a sudden blast of Tina Turner's "The Best", which shakes the room. I can't help it, giggles start somewhere in the pit of my stomach and bubble right up through my chest as Granny covers her ears and raises her eyebrows. The music is too loud, but it muffles the laughter and I risk turning my head. The groom, Sebastian, is a tall man in his late sixties. I've met him a few times but now I'm looking at him in a new light. Jacqui's been waving around the giant ring he gave her for months now. I remember that when his wife died he was devastated. Or was it all an act?

Could he have murdered her? Rebecca?

He walks down the aisle and stops at the end of our row of chairs. He's wearing a proper suit. Very nice. Very expensive. His shoes are so shiny they're reflecting the snow falling outside the window. The registrars smile at him and he smiles back. I must say, he looks incredibly nervous. I suppose I would if I was about to marry Jacqui. Tina Turner bops to a halt and a lone cello strikes up, played by a woman sitting in the corner. I hadn't noticed her before, but the sound is lovely. A violin joins in

141

and they play that tune – the one from the advert. The door at the back clicks open and we all turn our heads.

"Oh, lordy," says Granny.

Jacqui's dressed in green velvet. Head to toe, with a long train behind her. She's followed by a little girl who must be a relative, also dressed in green velvet. They're both wearing red crowns of holly and I have to say they look pretty fantastic. In a good way. Or at least the little girl does. She looks like a flower fairy and she's beaming from ear to ear. Jacqui looks slightly more like a table centrepiece, but when she stops and turns and smiles at people on our side of the aisle, her dress clings and swings and it does look good. Jacqui and the music move slowly until she gets to the front and everything goes quiet except for rustling and whispering. She's so close, I can smell her perfume. Her shoulders are joggling slightly and I wonder if she's got the giggles or is having a quiet sob. Sebastian squeezes her hand and Granny makes a little "Ah" sound next to me.

Now that everyone's staring at them, I take a chance to look at the rest of the crowd. I recognise doctors from the surgery and friends of Jacqui's that I've met, and also Anthony, Jacqui's son. He's looking even more uncomfortable than Lucas in his suit. With a bowl cut, his skin looks ultra pale with two big red spots where his cheekbones must be. He's wearing a red shirt that I bet was chosen by Jacqui. The little girl sits next to him; so cute.

The registrars are saying things of great significance that go straight past me and I can't help but stare out at the falling snow. It's slight, not at all blizzardy, but enough to make this magical. In the distance, a tiger wanders across the view. It doesn't look at all bothered by the snow.

Are Siberian tigers a thing?

"So now I think all the formalities are done with the exception of the signing of the register. Mrs Duncan? Would you like to go first?"

"Mrs Duncan! Oooh, yes, please," says Jacqui, and everyone laughs.

She leans forward to sign, and I look across at her new husband, who has stopped looking so terrified and is now smiling broadly. She stands back while the registrar blots the page. Jacqui hands Sebastian the big fountain pen and he steps forward.

"Here?" he asks.

"Yes." The registrar points at the book, next to Jacqui's signature. We're so close I can almost read it.

I lean right forward to look. Next to me, Lucas does the same.

The new husband pushes up his sleeve to sign with a big flourish.

I watch the pen, his hands, and then I spot something glittering.

There, around his wrist, is a thing like a charm bracelet, but instead of charms hang small teeth. Each one held by a golden ring.

I sit back, rattling my chair, banging into Lucas.

Next to me Lucas jumps. His eyes are saucer-wide.

Mum gets up and signs the register too.

The ceremony comes to an end, and everyone claps, music starts and there's hubbub all around us.

Mum, Granny and Paolo take glasses of champagne from waiters with trays.

Everyone mixes and chats.

But Lucas and I sit staring out of the window at the falling snow.

"What have we just seen?" he says eventually.

"I don't know," I whisper. "But Oskar's a total red herring."

Chapter 14

The food is sumptuous, and luckily we're put on a table with Mum and Granny and Paolo and some of the keepers from the estate.

There's a buffet so we're able to talk while loading our plates with salmon and potatoes and delicious salads that I'd fill my pockets with if I thought I could get away with it. Lucas takes three pieces of salmon. I raise my eyebrow at him. "I don't think anyone's going to care – I mean, look at it!" He's right. There's so much food it's almost obscene.

"Did you see if there was a gap on that bracelet?"

I mutter. "You know, one tooth missing. Could it be where the one I found came from?"

"I couldn't tell," he says.

I balance another potato on top of my plate and take it back over to the table. Granny's pinned one of the animal keepers to his chair and is asking all about dangerous animals.

"So what would you do if you were chased by a lion?"

The keeper laughs. "Oh, goodness! Well, die probably. Even our lions are still hunters at heart."

"Yes, but supposing you were caught — I don't know, in a car out there which had run out of petrol and there was no phone, no help. How would you avoid being killed? You must know. After all, you're a lion keeper."

"There are stun guns, of course. All over the park, just in case."

"How do those work?"

Getting up from the table I wander over to a waitress with a tray of sparkling drinks. "Champagne or elderflower?" she says. I'm tempted to take champagne but I know that Mum would disown me and leave me out for the fairies. I take a tall glass of elderflower and amble around the tables, finding the slowest and closest route to the top table.

Jacqui and Sebastian are sitting together. Along the table on one side are Anthony and the little girl. No sign of the little girl's mum. On the other side are two men holding hands, one of whom is definitely Sebastian's son, as he's got the same massive jaw. He's actually really good-looking. Perhaps to Jacqui, who is ancient, Sebastian is very good-looking. He's certainly very rich if the house is anything to go by.

I admire the centrepiece on the table opposite and crouch down as if I'm checking out the silver-sprayed fir cones. Looking up through the holly, I try to get a glance at his wrist, but apart from a massive gold watch I can't see anything, his cuffs come too low. I spend a few minutes poking the holly and berries until a waiter appears by my side. "You OK there, miss?"

"Oh!" I say, taking the opportunity to knock over my elderflower drink. "Oh no!"

Two waiters rush over with cloths and there's a kerfuffle, and Jacqui glances at me and so does

Sebastian. I get a really good stare in, but I still can't see his wrist properly and if I stare any more he'll think there's something wrong with me.

I fix a grin, apologise and head back over to our table with a new glass of elderflower. Granny's still cross-questioning the keeper, and Paolo and Mum are gazing into each other's eyes like sweethearts. What is it with weddings? Lucas, on the other hand is watching me.

"If you had to, then I'd suggest you stay still … or sing," says the keeper to Granny.

"Sing?" Granny laughs. "Is that a thing?"

"Has happened. Somewhere, I think." The keeper turns to Lucas for help, but Lucas swings round to me, turning his back on their conversation.

"Any luck?" he says.

There's a high-pitched pinging sound. It's Anthony, bashing his glass with a knife.

Lucas freezes. All heads turn to look at the top table. I keep my gaze glued to Sebastian's hand. I now can't remember which hand it was – right or left? Anthony takes a big breath and raises his glass. "To the bride and groom! My lovely mum Jacqui, and Sebastian – the happy couple."

"To Jacqui and Sebastian," choruses the entire room, and there's whooping and clinking of glasses and someone laughs and Jacqui looks so incredibly happy.

Mum blows Jacqui a kiss, and Jacqui catches her eye and winks back.

I watch as Jacqui links her arm through Sebastian's and they look into each other's eyes.

A friend of Sebastian's stands up and makes a short speech – perhaps he's the best man? He talks about how utterly reliable Sebastian is, what a great friend, a man of integrity.

Thinking about that toxicology report I'm not so sure he's right.

After that, it's time for pudding. While Granny and Paolo ogle the profiteroles, Lucas moves to sit beside me.

"I've been trying to get a look at his wrist," he says, "but I can't see a thing."

I pause, and for a moment I try to imagine the barriers that are stopping us taking a look at Sebastian's bracelet. Embarrassment, mainly.

"OK," I say. "I can fix this."

"Wha–?"

I dump my plate on the table and thread my way past the teetering piles of excessive puddingness until I'm standing right in front of Jacqui and Sebastian.

"So happy for you both," I say, and from behind the table Jacqui stands up, leans over and slaps a kiss on my cheek.

"Darling, it's so lovely to have you here to celebrate with us. Although I'm guessing it's pretty dull for someone of your age. Lots of old fossils like us."

"Oh no," I say. "It's lovely — so pleased to be asked. So much more fun than double maths, and look at the snow falling outside. Just magical."

Sebastian laughs. "Ordered it specially."

I giggle and then gasp. "Oh, wow!" I say, pointing at Sebastian's wrist. "That's a beautiful bracelet."

"Oh!' he says, pulling back his cuff.

"Are those human?" I ask, ducking my fingers under the cuff to check if there's an obvious gap on the chain. I actually manage to touch one of the teeth.

"Oh no, they're croc teeth," he laughs. "They were dug out of a branch when I was attacked in my twenties. The branch saved my life." He fends off an imaginary crocodile with a fork.

"Oh!" I say. "Ow!"

"It was ... painful. Worse for the croc though. See that?" He holds up his other hand and I can see a curved line down the side of his palm. "Bitten by a monkey too."

I must frown at him, because he laughs. "It's fine. Occupational hazard of running a safari park. You have to start somewhere and I started in Australia, where the animals are bigger and nastier than here, then worked in India for a while. Here at least they're all behind the wire."

"So you set the teeth in gold," I say.

"Yeah, all six of them. Worn it ever since."

"Wow," I say. "Amazing."

"Come on, darling, time to mingle," says Jacqui, sweeping Sebastian to his feet and heading off towards a raucous table of ancients. I watch them go.

Six teeth.

And all of them still there, looking just like the one we found.

So how does it add up? None missing from

his bracelet, and yet there's the one from the lay-by. And why wasn't he more bothered about me asking? If he's a murderer, I mean.

I shudder.

"You OK, poppet?" says Granny. "You look like you've just seen a ghost."

Chapter 15

The snow is heavy all the way back and we drive in tense silence. Mum's sleepy and Granny must be too because she nods off with her mouth open in the back of the car and puffs out little snores.

Paolo stares through the windscreen and the snow drives towards us like the credits at the beginning of *Star Wars*. Small drifts are forming along the side of the road and the lines in the middle have disappeared completely.

"It's a white-out," mumbles Lucas.

No one else says anything.

We slow for the roundabout, passing the cheery lights of a petrol station.

I hear Paolo breathe in, but not breathe out until we make it down a long curved hill past a tiny farmstead with cosy lights on inside. A few cars pass us going the other way, but we mostly have the road to ourselves.

It can't be more than about two miles, but the road goes on forever.

"Shall I turn off down through Freshford?" says Paolo.

"Go for the main hill," says Lucas. "Please."

He's right. The lanes through the village are narrow and steep.

Paolo sticks to the main road, but the snow's thicker on the brow of the hill and there's only one lane open in the middle of the road. We creep forward.

We're alone, until suddenly we're not. The first thing I notice is the lights burning in the back window. I turn my head a little, but I don't get to look backward because we're jolted forward, once, twice.

"What the—" shouts Mum.

We spin, and I feel the impact a third time, this time on Lucas's side.

"Whoa!" he shouts, and I lurch sideways, stopped from crushing Granny by the seatbelt.

But the person behind us hasn't finished; we're hit again from the rear. I bite my tongue and my mouth fills with blood.

Someone's screaming and I realise it's Granny. "Stop it!" she shouts. "Stop it!"

Paolo's fighting with the wheel, and we hit an enormous snowdrift.

"We're trapped!" shouts Lucas.

"This is not how I expected to die!" says Mum.

Headlights sweep the ceiling of the car.

Crunch.

Granny's window breaks and she's thrown across me as her door crumples.

"Oh! Oh!" she says. I grab her bony shoulders and pull her over my chest while bracing myself for another hit, but it doesn't come. Instead, more huge headlights appear from the other direction and the engine behind us roars. Tyres squeal and a tail of snow lashes our back window before the lights behind us swing away.

The windscreen wipers flash back and forth.

Paolo switches off the engine.

"Holy…" says Lucas.

A figure silhouetted by the headlights knocks on the window and Paolo opens his door.

"I saw that. Are you guys all OK?"

It's the beardy man from the petrol station at the bottom of the hill.

"Are we?" says Mum. "Are you, Paolo?"

Paolo is shaking. He crosses himself and says, "I'm fine." He obviously isn't.

Lucas mumbles something. Holds up his hand to the side of his face and checks his palm.

"Did you bang your head?" asks Granny.

"I thought so," says Lucas. "But no, I'm OK."

Granny nudges me. "All right, poppet?" she asks.

"I'm fine, Granny. Are you?" I say. But I'm not fine. I'm absolutely furious.

The man from the petrol station helps us get the car back on the road. Everyone but Granny pushes it out of the drift. It's absolutely freezing, my fingers burn cold on the outside of the car but we slide it from the verge, back on to where the tyre tracks show we must have slid off the road.

The garage man takes pictures on his phone and gives us his number as a witness. "I'd call the police," he says, "but they're not going to come out in a hurry; you'd freeze to death waiting. You OK getting home from here?"

"Thank you so much," says Mum. "We can limp back." She puts the car in gear and with the snow still driving at the windscreen we creep down the hill.

Slowly we make it to the traffic lights and Mum turns right, skidding slightly sideways towards the top of our road. A car, stuck on the hill, has been abandoned, lights flashing, and Mum pauses a moment. "What do you think? Should we try it?" she says.

"S'up to you," says Paolo.

"I don't mind walking," says Granny. "Rather be cold than dead."

Really carefully, Mum turns off the road into the canal basin car park. Here the snow is thick and untouched and she's able to turn and park the car properly. It's a mile uphill to our house, but I agree with Granny and it turns out that Paolo, used to his mountainous Italian village, has packed the boot of the car with coats and blankets and wellies. Mum togs up Granny and they set off up towards the canal towpath, Mum on one side, Paolo on the other.

Lucas and I dress ourselves hurriedly in the weird things that are left. A woolly coat of Mum's and a leather jacket thing belonging to Paolo. My boots are too big; Lucas's too small. He tries to slam the boot shut, but it pings half open again. I stand for a moment to look at the car. It looks all right from the front, but the back and sides are punched in, like some giant took a swing at us.

"We were lucky," says Lucas. "We should have been killed. That was a Land Rover that hit us. Massive. Built like a tank."

I glance back towards the main road. "I think we need to get going." I follow the others up on to the towpath.

"Do you think they'll come back?" asks Lucas.

"They can't drive along here," I say. "But..."

It's dark, but the snow's reflecting all the light there is so we can see quite easily.

"So we rattled someone," he says as we wade

through the snow.

"Sebastian," I say. "Although he did a good job of not looking bothered."

"He did, didn't he. But I bet he owns one of those giant cars."

"He must be really worried. He left his own wedding to drive us off the road."

"That is like … immense."

We trudge on, passing through woodsmoke from the narrowboats moored along the canal. Some of them look closed up, but one or two have yellow lit windows, warm and cosy, like something from a little kid's picture book.

The snow falls so thickly all around us, I begin to relax.

"So what's happened to Oskar?" I step in a concealed puddle, shooting icy water up my legs. "Whoa!"

"Holiday?" says Lucas.

"He'd have told Mum. He'd have said something on Sunday. He's just disappeared."

Lucas stops to shake the snow from a branch and it flumps on to the ground. "What are you thinking?"

"He might have stolen the money from the surgery. But he wouldn't have killed Dr Price, or Sebastian's first wife, nor was he driving that car. He can't drive, for a start. I'm thinking that far from being the murderer, he – well…"

We walk on in silence. Ahead of us Mum shouts to say they've reached the road and that they're going up the hill.

"He's not at home. His social media accounts have gone dead." Lucas pauses. "He was on to something, wasn't he. Maybe he knew more than we realised."

"Perhaps he confronted Sebastian," I say, stopping. I remember the awful crunching sound as the big car hit us and try to shake it out of my head, listening instead to the now sounds. The snow continues to fall around us, pittering, pecking the leaves, skittering across the frozen canal. It's comforting, but also kind of eerie. "But the police are banking on it being him. Mum said they've stopped looking for anyone else."

We walk on. Reaching the bottom of the hill we pass another abandoned car. Up the hill I can hear Granny's laugh, and Mum hoots. I'm guessing

Paolo's fallen down or someone's got snow down the back of their necks. It's good to hear them laugh, but I'm worried that they're not taking it all seriously enough. As I put one foot in front of another that feeling of dread seeps back into my stomach.

Chapter 16

After Mum and Paolo have rung the police, who say they'll "look into it", we have a weird evening that feels fuelled by false jollity. The fire, the falling snow, spiced apple juice to drink and grins pasted on all our faces. Being "rammed" in the car turns to the "accident" until I almost believe it myself, but no matter how many games we play and how much we laugh, I feel sick. The snow is making it worse. We're trapped, and I can't help imagining there's someone out there. I stand at the window, peering into the dark garden.

Mum comes to stand beside me. She looks a little sad. "Going to miss Jacqui and Oskar."

"But he's a murderer, dear," says Granny from the sofa. "Can you miss a murderer?"

"Yeah, but," says Mum. "He was lovely for all that." She stares out into the dark with a faraway look. Then frowns. I don't think she believes that Oskar's a murderer any more than I do. But I won't say anything. I don't want to worry her.

Later, on the landing, when I've come out of the bathroom, Lucas hisses from his doorway and I slip into his room. It smells slightly. Actually quite a bit, but it's tidy. Thinking about it, mine probably smells too.

"Look what I've found."

Lucas holds out his phone. There's a picture of Sebastian and another woman. Taken somewhere sunny.

"Who's this?"

"His wife. His first wife. Rebecca. And look, close up – here."

Lucas expands the picture and I peer at the couple. "What am I looking at?"

"Round her neck."

"Oh!"

I take the phone from him and zoom in on the photo with my fingers. There, hanging from a gold chain, is another tooth. Again, it's set in gold. This time it's hanging free and on its own. "It could be…" I say. "It really could."

"I bet it is," he says.

I stare at the picture. It does look like the tooth. If I hadn't hidden it at Granny's I could compare it. "What are you thinking?"

"I'm wondering if Sebastian wore this one…" he jabs the screen, "when he was disposing of the body, and somehow it got caught and pinged off or something and ended up on the hill. Your mum probably mentioned to Jacqui that you'd found it, and she would have told Sebastian. Plus he probably knows that you and I have the letter, the toxicology report. I bet it was him in the market – he probably followed us all the way from school, to the garages and then into town."

"And then he tried to ram us – to kill us?"

"But this picture is proof that the tooth is connected to him. And that letter is definitely connected to him."

"I wish we still had that letter. What are we going to do?"

Lucas pushes his phone back into his pocket. "I have absolutely no idea."

I don't really sleep. Instead I worry. What's happened to Oskar? Is he stuck in a box somewhere on the side of the road? Tossing and turning, I think back to his phone call on the first night. He had suspicions – he wanted to talk to Mum about them but stuff happened. What happened? Jacqui happened. He didn't get to come over on his own. She came too. Did he not want to talk in front of her? I picture the scene, Oskar standing in the kitchen in his hand-knit sweater, Mum and Jacqui chatting. Him suggesting that Dr Price spotted something in the records.

He was one hundred per cent correct as it happens.

And he never got to finish what he was going to say. I wonder what more he would have said. Did he know about that letter?

I turn over again.

He would know Sebastian. He could have seen Sebastian play the grieving widower and seen that Jacqui's a sucker for a sob story.

The moment I hear Mum's alarm go off I get up. It's blue-black outside, and the snow has stopped. She'll be leaving for work soon and I want to catch her before she does.

Downstairs I feed Garibaldi and let him out the back door into the snow. He stands and stares at the shelf of white that's appeared outside. "Go on, scaredy-cat," I say gently, nudging him out. Something moves in the snow shade of a bush and he leaps off to kill it.

I put on the kettle and look out at the countryside all white and untouched. Nothing has driven along the lane this morning, but as I stare, a blue tractor loaded with hay steams up the hill. OK, fair enough. Tractors. How long before cars, I wonder?

Mum appears fully dressed at the bottom of the stairs. "Oh, Rube, I thought you'd still be in bed. Lie-in and all that after yesterday's excitement. I've got a four-wheel drive booked for ten minutes' time to get me to work." She looks up at the clock and drops her phone in her handbag.

"Thought I'd get up and enjoy the snow."

"Oh?" she says, raising an eyebrow. "You never normally miss an opportunity for a lie-in. Anyway, I can meet the police by the car later – show them the damage AND get to work. They've said they reckon it was a joy-rider – stolen car, having fun in the snow, getting out of control on the slippery roads."

"Really?" I say. "You believe that?"

"Yeah, apparently it's quite common." She jams a piece of bread in the toaster. "Anyway, I don't want to think about it."

"Mum," I say, ladling tea leaves into the pot. "Did you ever meet Sebastian's wife?"

"Rebecca? Oh, yes. She used to come to the surgery until she became so ill that Dr Price went out to her. We all delivered medicines on occasion. But it was so sad."

"Uh-huh?" I dig around in the kitchen drawer for a strainer. "So her death was – expected?"

"Well, yes, but it came much sooner than they'd thought. I seem to remember she died over a weekend. Dr Price was surprised – he'd thought she'd last longer, poor thing. Seb went on visiting the surgery after she died. So miserable, he was just so terribly sad, until Jacqui, you know…"

I reach into the fridge for the milk. "And was his wife rich?"

"Rich?"

"Yeah. Like, was he the one with all the money or was she?"

"Oh, goodness, I don't know. He's the one with the title, but titles don't always mean riches. Places like that cost a fortune to run."

"Ah – of course. Tea?"

While Paolo walks Granny home and says he'll walk back down to the canal basin to see if our car is driveable, I spend the morning waiting for Lucas to get out of bed. I drag a plastic sledge from the shed and take a couple of swoops down the hill above the house, but my heart's not in it. Back inside I learn every single line of every single song in *Hairspray*. Mostly in a desperate attempt to forget about last night. I'm really aware that if Sebastian wants to find us, he knows exactly where we are. He knows that Mum will have gone to the surgery – and that our car is probably dead. He doesn't know if the police have taken any action and I cling to the hope that he might think they're keeping us under surveillance or something like that. Essentially, I'm caught between terrified, angry and worried. And every time I hear a car, my heart rate bumps and my mouth goes dry.

The snow begins again, slowly this time, feathery, turning in the headlights of the few cars on the lane, but not settling.

I type a message to Mia. *If anything happens to me. The tooth is at Granny's in Mum's old room in a shell box.*

Lol. Drama queen, she types. *Wanna talk?*

But I don't, and I keep on singing the songs and practising the steps until Lucas knocks on my door, and I feel oddly relieved. "News?" he asks.

"Mum's gone to work, Granny's gone home with Paolo. Oh, and Mum said Dr Price was surprised that Rebecca Duncan Smith died so quickly."

Lucas raises an eyebrow.

"I also asked if his wife had lots of money." I watch a car creep along the lane. "But Mum didn't know. She did say that house would take a lot of cash to keep running though."

Lucas smiles. "That's it! He definitely bumped

her off so that he could inherit all her cash – but got caught out by Dr Price. We'd have the proof if we could find the letter. Do you think your mum would believe you without it?"

I shake my head. "No, she'd just tell me I had an overactive imagination. Your dad? Would Paolo believe you?"

"Not a chance without that toxicology report."

We both stare out at the snow.

"There'd be more proof in their house," I say.

I hear Lucas swallow. "Darkwood?"

"Yeah." My mouth is now so dry I can barely speak.

"Sorry? Are you suggesting…?"

"I am."

"Are they going on a honeymoon? We could – like, go then?"

"They're going to Africa on a safari next week, but that might be too late. He might … stay there, or murder Jacqui or – I don't know."

"You want to find out now."

"I do."

He stares at me for a long time. "You've got guts," he says.

I feel unreasonably happy when he says it.

He drops to a crouch and sits in the doorway, his back against the landing wall. "Ruby, I've got to come clean. You know when we walked back that night and found Dr Price in the box…"

"What?" I wait.

"I wanted you to open it."

"I think I knew that."

"I'd been looking at it for four days. I was sure – so sure that he was in there. But I didn't expect him to fall out of it. I didn't think it would be – traumatic."

"How did you know he was in there?" I say eventually.

"I've no idea. I just thought it was odd the way he disappeared, and then this big box appeared. And it was the right size and so … I put the owl on it."

"That's you? The mysterious tagger?"

He nods.

"That is…" I am lost for words.

He breathes in and out. "I feel better now," he says. "I needed to tell you."

He looks almost happy so I risk it. "Would you come with me?"

"Tomorrow?" he says.

I nod.

"I thought you'd never ask."

Chapter 17

I'm feeling everything now. Definitely unreasonably warm and squishy that Lucas has trusted me with his graffiti secret – me, of all the people in the world; slightly peeved that he tricked me into opening the cabinet; and sick to my boot soles about my resolution to go to Darkwood House.

My arms and legs are leaden, my tongue sticking to the roof of my mouth. "How are we going to do this? Do you think we should climb in through a window? Or what?"

"If he's a killer, I'd suggest we don't."

"The tooth's still at Granny's."

"Oh!" he says. "You mean he won't kill us until he knows where the tooth is?"

"If we don't come back, Mia knows where it is."

He nods. I see the Adam's apple in his neck go up and down as he tries to swallow. So the dread isn't just me then.

For the second night I don't actually sleep.

Well, perhaps I do. I don't think I lie awake for eight hours. Between dozes I think of ways to convince Mum, but she always thinks the best of people and I can't work out a way to get her onside about Sebastian. As a result the dread stays exactly where it is.

The road's clear now. Lumps of blackened ice line the sides and the pavement has become a toboggan run. The buses are running though, so we can still get there. I dress slowly, wondering what part of me thought this was a good idea. Two pairs of socks. A vest. All the clothes that Granny would approve of and Trixie Thompson would scoff at.

"We thought we'd go to see the animals, and maybe stay on for the lights, at Darkwood," I say to

Mum. She's doing an online order on her laptop.

"Can't give you a lift, I'm afraid. The car's been towed off to be fixed. The police are going to take a look at it too. They think it was a joy rider, out of control. Hoping we might get a hire car by tomorrow." I can feel the happiness coming off her and she grabs me, pulling me close. "So relieved all that nastiness is over, and the wedding was just the icing on the cake."

"Mum, do you really believe that the car was just a joy rider?"

"That's what the police said."

"You don't think it was deliberate — someone trying to kill us?"

"Don't be silly, darling. Why would anyone want to kill us?"

"Because, because we know things about Dr Price — about Sebastian's first wife..." There, now I've said it.

"We know that Seb's first wife died of cancer, and that he loved her very much, and now he loves Jacqui and that's just lovely. The rest — oh, Ruby, you always did have an overactive imagination." She kisses me on the top of my head.

"Yeah, well," I say non-committally. "So we'll see you later."

"I'm glad you're both going together." Mum smiles. "Paolo will be delighted."

We do exactly as we said we would. We catch the bus into town with all the old people with drippy noses, who steam up the windows. On the way we buy ourselves eye wateringly expensive tickets to the safari park. And then we wait for the special bus that goes down to Darkwood. That's full of families, overexcited little kids and panicky parents. Lucas and I take the last two seats and sit crammed up against a small child who offers me Hula Hoops from his finger, which he sucks each time he plunges it back into the bag. "Nice," says Lucas.

The little minibus races along the main road, passing the place where the car rammed us, where the carriageway goes down to a single lane. Grubby banks of snow line the way, but the cars and our minibus whizz along as if it was high summer. The sky is heavy and almost yellow.

"Gonna snow again," says Lucas pointing up.

After a couple of miles, the bus turns right through the main gates and we wind along the driveway. This isn't the way we came the other day. I turn my phone over in my pocket and gaze out at the wildebeest.

Lucas rubs at his right eye and I notice white paint on his thumbnail.

"Why do you always paint an owl?" I ask.

"The owl is a symbol of wisdom," he says.

"They're nice. Good design," I say.

"Thanks," he says, and a small smile flickers in his cheek.

The minibus thumps to a halt and before the door opens the boy next to me has scrabbled from his seat and run for the exit. "Stop, Wilf!" shouts his mother.

"'Scuse me," she says, scrambling past, whacking the side of my head with her elbow and rushing after her son.

Lucas and I are the last to get off. We stand uncertainly in the car park.

"Now what?" he says. "How are we going to get into the house?"

There's no actual fence, but five people in dayglo

tabards are each stationed on one of the paths leading up to the house. "Dunno. Do you think it'll be easier when it's dark?"

Lucas flips his phone open. "That's ages though. We'll have to think of a way."

"OK, so we're going to go round the scary men, right to the front door…"

"… ring the bell…"

"…say we happened to come down, and wanted to say thank you very much…"

"…they'll invite us in…"

"One of us looks for Sebastian's office?"

"Keeping our eyes on the exit – so that we can run, if necessary, but Jacqui will be there too, so we'll be perfectly fine."

"Or we climb in through a window and we both search the house and hope we're not spotted. Easy-peasy."

"Good," says Lucas. "That's sorted. Now, can we just go and look at the zebras?"

There's snow on the ground, but someone's salted it, so the main thoroughfare has turned to slush. Thick snow sits on the huts selling chips and doughnuts and it starts to fall again, dusting the slush with white so that it all begins to look rather magical. The red pandas coil up around each other for warmth and their furry russet bodies are beautiful against the white. Someone turns the fairy lights on and although it's not dark, the place goes all twinkly. Masses of little warm yellow dots peek from dense hedges, and tall spikes of ridiculously overdressed Christmas trees loom over every wall. The house itself is lit in multicoloured washes from giant spotlights, as are some of the majestic trees. As we stand, watching the lights come into their own, the snow puts on a surge, brushing my cheeks and melting.

The yellow sky disappears and everything goes snowy. I suppose it's still broad daylight, but it's December and broad daylight is hanging back.

Everywhere we go we're accompanied by a faint rattling. I finally work it out. Even here, Lucas has his spray can.

"You're not thinking of tagging anything here, I hope?" I say.

"No, don't be daft, I only tag ugly things. You know, parts of the services infrastructure –

electricity substations, telephone connection boxes, fire hydrants."

"And bodies in boxes."

He laughs. "That too. I really am dead sorry, you know. I should have looked myself, but I was ... scared, I guess."

We buy some overpriced cheesy chips and watch a small child have a total meltdown over a doughnut. The snow changes to thick and feathery and the light drops another degree.

"What do you reckon?" asks Lucas. "Visibility's rubbish."

"Perfect. Let's go now, walk through the maze over there and see if we can get as near to the house as possible."

We join the patchy groups of families heading for the maze, lose our way and end up in the stable courtyard that adjoins the house. "Yes!" says Lucas as we join the mass of people around a huge tree that's playing Mariah Carey and hohoho-ing on a loop tape. Lights dance across the windows, all of which are closed, with blinds or shutters behind reflecting stories of sleighs and snowflakes. It would look better in the dark, but it does do a

Christmas thing in the snow. I wonder how tacky it would be *without* the snow.

A small child wearing an enormous bobble hat is running round and round the tree in the middle. Everyone's watching him.

"We could get through one of those windows," says Lucas.

"You might," I say, looking up at him. "But I'm about a foot too short to reach, and I think we'd just end up inside the stables. And everyone can see us."

Ahead of us is another exit from the main courtyard. A few stragglers are heading away from the laughing tree and we follow until we're on a terrace, right by the house, listening to hits from Queen's back catalogue and dodging purple searchlights. The snow's falling heavily through the purple lights and it deadens all the sounds, even Freddie Mercury.

I pull my hood right over my head. The snowflakes are clinging to the fur on the front. Carefully I shake the furry edge, and in the process my gloves turn from navy to white.

"I think we should find somewhere to shelter

while we decide what we're going to do," says Lucas.

The nearest thing is the shade of a giant hedge. As we stand with our backs to it, it gives us the opportunity to stare at the house.

The front terrace is huge windows, blank and unapproachable. It has a door that's shockingly public. "No way am I going up there to try the door," I say. "Let's find a more private entrance. Maybe the one we used when we went to the wedding?"

Lucas nods, and when the snow lets up a little we go on round the corner.

Beyond the terrace is a maze of low hedges with illuminated mushrooms all over it. It's also patrolled by two people in dayglo vests.

"Do you think we could just talk to them, tell them we're friends of Jacqui and Sebastian's?"

"No," says Lucas. "They've got walkie-talkies where they ought to have hearts. I vote we sneak past them. Going to be easier."

"We could just ask Jacqui to find us more proof."

"Maybe that's plan B."

I look over the field of strange little talking mushrooms. Perhaps they're not mushrooms.

Perhaps they're potatoes.

"Hopeless," says Lucas. "Better in the first courtyard."

I don't say anything. I'm kind of hoping that we can't get in at all. Then we could just go home and stick our heads under the duvets and hope the whole thing will go away.

Except it won't. Sebastian tried to kill us.

Sebastian will try to kill us again.

We have to stop him killing more people. If Mum and the police don't think anything's wrong then it's up to us to get more proof, and getting into the house is our best hope.

I feel sick.

Chapter 18

Halfway through the mushroom field, the path veers into a hedge-walled garden with long strings of blue lights in lines along the ground. There are no people in high-vis vests here. No other tourists.

Without giving myself a chance to think about it, I run towards the house. "Hey!" hisses Lucas behind me, but I don't look back and keep running until I can stop behind a tree. Lucas crashes in behind me. I glance back. A family have stopped to take pictures of the lights, but there are no officials that I can see. We're about halfway to the house and

I can see that there's a low wall at the end. Perfect.

I sidle the rest of the way, my back to the hedge, keeping my feet clear of the first string of lights. I don't want anyone to wonder why the lights flash on and off as my foot covers them. The line of lights stops a metre before the wall and in happy snow cover I clamber over the wall and stop to take my breath on the other side.

"Whoa!" says Lucas. "I've never done anything like that before – not in real life."

Nor have I, I think. It's kind of buzzy. But so far we've been lucky.

A narrow strip of paving runs along the side of the house. All the hedges and garden stop well away from the building itself and this low wall seems to run with the paving. Someone must have swept the snow from it earlier but there are a couple of centimetres that have fallen in the last half-hour and it's cold. I look at the knees of my jeans. They're already wet. Dropping to my hands and knees, I creep forward until we leave the blue-lined garden and emerge into one full of huge angel wings in white. Again, we're behind the wall and now, a few metres in front of me, I can see a door that looks like the one in the room where the marriage took place.

Lucas taps my leg and points to the door. The only thing I can see of him is his face, but I think I can smell his fear. Or is that me?

The snow chooses that moment to really chuck it down.

It's a sign. The door looks promising, but the wall dies a couple of metres away. We'd be in full sight of the angel garden, if anyone was there. And what if the door's locked?

It's not like you don't know Jacqui, I say to myself. Although if we're spotted we'll be dragged away by the heavies and it'll take ages to get back to the house.

A family over in the angel garden are taking selfies, with camera flashes; they're laughing about being in a real snow globe. This is my chance.

Stuffing my fear into my shoes I straighten up and, stepping over a low chain that crosses the path, walk purposefully over to the door. I press down the handle and give the door a push. It doesn't move. No!

I give it a gentle shove with my shoulder and this

time it opens.

I step through into a low-lit hallway, Lucas crams in behind me and we close the door and stop.

"Now what?" he whispers.

"I don't know. I didn't think we'd get in. I thought we'd have to knock and talk to Jacqui. Now it's like we've broken in. And we're not where I thought we were."

We really aren't. This is not the wedding room, this is a boot-filled corridor. Doggy and muddy. All that marks it out as belonging to a mansion are the antlers that are pretending to be coat hooks.

"OK – so either sneak on in or we run away."

I remember Granny saying that it's the things we didn't do that bug us in later life. "I vote we go on," I say, not believing it myself.

"'K," mutters Lucas behind me.

Looking down at the melting pools of ice we've left in the doorway, I wonder if we should take off our shoes, but that would make it difficult to run. I keep my boots on. They aren't mine, they're Mum's, and I'm hoping they'll give me some of her confidence.

"Lead the way then," Lucas says.

At the end of the passage is a door with light showing underneath.

I stop with my hand on the doorknob and glance back at Lucas. "Yes?" I say.

"Yup."

I turn the handle and push the door open, yanking a smile on to my face just in case.

It takes a moment for me to understand the room. It's so big, and the furniture is so large that at first I don't spot the people in it. It's the perfume that greets me first.

"Ruby, sweetie, what a lovely surprise." Jacqui's sitting in front of a huge fireplace, her feet tucked up next to her on the armchair.

"Jacqui!" I say, stepping into the room and only then spotting the other person, Sebastian.

Sebastian heaves himself to his feet and smiles broadly.

"Lucas too. Darlings, how lovely, but how did you get in?" asks Jacqui. "Security are supposed to keep people out, not that it isn't wonderful to see you."

"We walked past them," I lie. Behind me, Lucas coughs. A laugh?

"My my, how lovely," says Sebastian, his forehead crinkling. "But why not call first? We could have given you a guided tour."

"It was a spur-of-the-moment thing," says Lucas. "See the lights in the snow. Visit the zebras, you know…"

I nod. "And then we just thought we'd see if you were in."

It sounds so weak, I can't believe they're believing us.

"Well, you're here now, so let's get you a hot chocolate or something, shall we?" Jacqui shoves her feet into some leopard-print slippers that I really hope aren't real fur and swooshes towards us. "Follow me. I think I know the way to the kitchen now," she laughs.

I laugh. Lucas laughs. Our laughs echo in the enormous room. Two dogs and a person follow us. I glance round. It's Sebastian. It's a total disaster.

Neither of us is going to get a chance to look for anything.

"Now, hot chocolate. Where would I find that?" Jacqui leads us into a vast kitchen, in the middle of which is a huge table. It's kind of old-fashioned.

Wooden and worn, and much colder than the room with the fire. She starts opening cupboards and Sebastian glides past to the giant fridge. He empties a bottle of milk into a pan and crashes it on to a stove at the side of the room, where it spits and bounces.

I watch him move. He seems very chill, not at all like a serial killer. But perhaps he's a psychopath and isn't bothered by the death toll he's leaving behind. Jacqui's still opening cupboards; she seems very relaxed too. Perhaps all I can do is warn her that she's living with a murderer. All this goes through my head in slow seconds, and I suspect I'm standing there with my mouth open because Lucas nudges me and I'm suddenly drawn back into the room.

"Thank you, that's really kind. Anyway, lots of visitors out there today," I say, looking round at Lucas desperately.

His eyes flash wide and he says, "Yes, really impressive, and the animals are great…"

"Good, good," says Sebastian, reaching up to get two mugs out of a cupboard. "Lovely to see the families enjoying themselves."

This is so awkward. So stupid. We should have climbed in through a window.

Or caused a distraction outside.

We should not have done this.

We stand there in the doorway as the milk comes to the boil and Sebastian pours it over the chocolate powder. Jacqui looks to me, to Lucas and back to me. She raises an eyebrow. I make a decision, smiling broadly back at her and tipping my head ever so slightly.

She takes the hint and whisks me round, shoving Lucas back into the kitchen. "C'mon, darling, tell me what you made of the wedding, did you like my dress? Sebastian, lovey, I'll have a coffee. Find some biscuits too. Lucas'll help you bring them in."

Lucas shoots me a death glare but I leg it down the passage towards the big sitting room, Jacqui at my heels. Once we're a few metres away from the kitchen and I can hear the rumble of Lucas and Sebastian talking, I whisper to Jacqui, "We were nearly killed on our way back the other night."

"Sally said you'd had an accident. I was worried about everyone setting off home afterwards in all that snow."

"It wasn't an accident, someone rammed us."

Jacqui stops, her mouth falls open. "For real?"

"Yeah. They definitely tried to kill us, all of us, my entire family."

"Who? Who would do that? Oskar?"

"It can't be Oskar, can it? He doesn't drive."

Jacqui looks down at the tiled floor, shaking her head. "He doesn't, no. Were you all OK? Your poor granny."

I nod my head. "She was just shaken, really." I stop and pull her close. "But the thing is, Jacqui, we think Sebastian..."

"What?"

"We think..." How can I tell her that her husband's a murderer? "We think he might be..."

"What is it, dear?"

Lucas and Sebastian appear in the corridor behind us and I stop. "Involved. You know..."

Jacqui frowns, but bundles me into the sitting room and behind the door.

"In Dr Price's murder."

"Don't be silly," she laughs. "Seb? You're imagining things, lovey."

"I've got proof, on my phone." I scrabble it out

193

of my pocket and hit the photo app.

Lucas and Sebastian swing round the door and land four mugs on the table.

"OK?" asks Sebastian, as Jacqui and I peer at the phone screen.

"Yup," I say. "Just showing Jacqui some pictures of the wedding."

"Marvellous, splendid," says Sebastian. "Now, Lucas – it is Lucas, isn't it? How much do you know about okapi?"

Lucas mumbles something about knowing nothing as I flick through the pics on the screen. Jacqui leans over my shoulder, looking keenly, and then I get to the picture of the tooth charm. "See, there," I say.

"Oh, that's lovely," she says, peering at the screen. I see her face as she registers what she's looking at. Momentarily she blenches, coughs and asks, "What is it?"

"A tooth. Found it on the hill," I murmur. "Near the ... near Dr..."

"Goodness." She hands the phone back to me. "But I'm not sure it proves anything."

"I think it does," I say.

"Seb?" she mouths. "No. You've got the wrong idea. Surely."

I don't reply, just mime the bracelet around my wrist, widen my eyes and put the phone back in my pocket.

"I think I need to see it in the flesh, as it were," she says.

I nod.

"Bring it over some time soon," she says.

I nod again.

"Good girl," she says, patting me on the back and handing me a lukewarm mug of hot chocolate. I gulp it down.

"But you're OK?"

"Having a ball," she says, hugging me and enveloping me in her perfume. "Anyway, you should get home. The last bus goes at six o'clock so you'd better make sure you can get back. Don't want you wandering around the safari park in the dark!"

"I'll give them a lift," says Sebastian, standing and patting his pockets. "Now, where are my car keys?"

"Oh no, honestly," I say. "I don't want to put you to any trouble."

"No trouble, no trouble at all, or it wouldn't be if I had any idea what I'd done with the keys. Haven't driven the darn thing since before the wedding. Jacqueline? Any idea?"

"You'd forget your head, Seb. They must be upstairs somewhere." She squeezes his arm but pulls away a little when he reaches out to hug her. He looks surprised. She glances over to me and swings her gaze towards the front of the house.

"Don't worry, we'll catch the bus; we can take a look at the lights. We've got ages," says Lucas, shrugging his coat back on and heading for the corridor we arrived down.

"I'll show them the short cut," says Sebastian. "You can walk through the woods down to the main road without going all the way along the drive."

"Short cut?" asks Lucas. "Aren't there tigers everywhere?"

Sebastian laughs. "Not everywhere – you just have to know the ways through. You don't want to end up as dinner, now, do you?"

"I'll show them," says Jacqui, flashing me a significant look. "I know the safe ways."

"Of course you do, darling. Well, goodbye. Bon voyage and take care." Sebastian smiles and, whistling to himself, pads up the stairs.

Jacqui watches him go. "You know, I understand exactly where you're coming from with that tooth thingy. I've seen him wear the bracelet and he has a necklace too…" She looks up the stairs behind him. "I wonder…" She steps towards the front door and her hand rests on the handle. "Why would he – you know … Dr Price?"

"Because Dr Price suspected that Sebastian's first wife was poisoned," hisses Lucas. "But we need more proof."

"Oh?"

"We've obviously got the tooth, and there is … was a letter," I whisper. "But we wondered if you could find out anything else."

"A letter that you have?"

"Kind of," says Lucas. "But the tooth's stowed away carefully."

"So where did you put it that's really safe. Not at home?"

I shake my head. "No."

She smiles. "At school?"

I shake my head again. "Granny's," I say.

Jacqui's mouth drops open, but then she raises her head, looking over my shoulder with a fixed grin on her face.

"I was going to say – you need the pass codes," says Sebastian from behind me. "One-nine-five-four. Works on all the gates."

He's standing right there. He'll have heard.

"Thank you, Sebastian," I say.

He coughs, somehow awkwardly, and shuffles his feet. "Ah, good. As I say – happy travels."

We all watch again as he climbs the stairs and then listen for him closing the door.

"So is the short cut safe?" says Lucas.

"Of course it is," says Jacqui, taking us sideways from the front door and instead leading us through the room with the giant Christmas tree. "Brrr," she says, opening the door that leads into the smaller car park. "There you are, dears."

"Thank you, Jacqui. Sorry to barge in earlier," I say. "And sorry about…" How do I say sorry for pointing the finger at your brand-new husband for being a murderer?

"Thank you, darling – I'll think on it. And it's

always a pleasure to see your smiling face." She kisses me on the cheek. "Anyway, you can either catch the bus from over there at the car park, but there might be a little wait, or, if you cut down to the main road on Seb's short cut, you're practically home."

"How do we do that?" asks Lucas.

"Hop over this fence here, on the left. You'll walk through the reindeer thingies, they're fine. Then if you pop up to the right, there's some big gates. Put the code in – one-nine-five-four, remember; it's Seb's birth year – and you can walk down that track. It takes you straight to Midford – you could just walk home from there."

"Thanks. And, Jacqui … do take care. I still—"

"Don't you worry, my love, I'm on top of it. I'll do a little digging."

I kiss her cheek. It's dusty with powder and smells like Jacqui always smells.

"Take care, darlings." She blows us another kiss and starts to close the door. "And looking forward to seeing you both in *Hairspray*."

"That'd be lovely. Mum'll get tickets."

We step out on to the fresh snow, our boots

making new tracks. Over to our right are a few cars. One of them is Jacqui's – a small red Nissan.

I look up, snow slowly swirling in the huge purple floodlights and see Jacqui looking out at us from the window.

She waves. I wave. And as we turn away I catch sight of the big car parked beyond Jacqui's. It's a massive Land Rover, the kind of thing the royal family drive. Although it's covered in snow, I can see that the front's all bashed. Like it might recently have had a brush with another car.

Chapter 19

We walk six paces from the house.

I look back again. Jacqui's gone.

"Why did you tell her where it really was?"

"Granny's?" I say. "I know I shouldn't have done. But look — look at that car."

I check the windows again. No sign of Jacqui or Sebastian. "C'mon," I say, trotting over the fresh snow and crouching behind Jacqui's little hatchback.

"You're right," he says, wiping a chunk of snow from the front bumper. "Look — blue paint."

"Mum's car," I say. "That proves it."

We scuttle around the far side. There are more bashes, now collecting snow but still, incriminating. "I wish Mum could see this," I say. "Actually..." I take my phone out of my pocket and set it to camera.

"The flash'll show from the house," says Lucas.

"I'll take that chance," I say, clicking the shutter twice. Each time, the car, the snow, the trees above us light up with the flash.

I look back towards the house. One of the upstairs curtains falls back into place.

"Let's get going. But why did you say it?"

"You mean Granny?"

"Yeah – I'm sure he heard."

Our feet are muffled by the snow.

"D'you really think so?"

"I do," says Lucas.

We stamp on through the steadily falling snow.

He's totally right. I'm in denial. Sebastian will have heard me say Granny's. He's only got to ask Jacqui where she lives and he'll pile on over.

"I'm such an idiot."

"You panicked. I might have said the same," says

Lucas. "I was about to say we'd hidden it under a table in Costa or somewhere. We need to get there ASAP."

"Or ring someone," I say, pulling my phone out of my pocket. "What do I say though?"

"Do you think we should take the bus? It might be quicker than walking," Lucas asks, shivering, turning his face towards the enormous car park where the bus stop is. The Christmas tree thing is still hohoho-ing and there are families wandering in the garden.

I press the button that says "MUM".

It rings. And rings, and then goes to voicemail. I can't think of a message, so I just press the red button and put the phone back in my pocket.

A second later, and it rings back.

"Mum," I say.

"Ruby, darling, how are you? Are you having a lovely time?"

"Oh, fine, it's just— Is Granny OK?"

"As far as I know, why?"

I take a deep breath and gabble. "It's just that Sebastian might be – like I said before – he might not be good, and we might have told him that

203

Granny's got the tooth charm and he's got a four-wheel drive that might have possibly been the one that drove us off the road. There's blue paint on the bumper — so actually it has to be him. I've got a pic."

"Ruby, sweetness, what have you done? Drunk too much coffee? You don't make any sense. Sebastian? Lovely Sebastian who just married Jacqui?"

"I'll send you the picture of his car. It's covered in your car's paint."

"Just get home, darling — there's a delicious hot pot thing that Paolo's made. Come back and we can all enjoy it together."

And the call ends.

I look down at the phone. It's trying to send the picture but the signal's minuscule.

"She didn't believe you?" says Lucas. "Is there any point in you ringing your granny? Warning her?"

"I think the reception might have died, but I'll try," I say, switching the light right down on my phone and pressing in the numbers for Granny.

After two attempts the phone rings.

And rings.

She doesn't answer.

"Do you think she's there?" asks Lucas.

"I don't know where else she'd be. Thick snow — she'll be tucked up with the exercise bike and the telly."

"On full volume," says Lucas.

I try again, imagining the phone ringing in the empty kitchen. There's no way she'll hear it.

"What about her mobile?"

"She switches it off when she's at home." I put the phone back in my pocket and we break into a run.

We jog without talking to the edge of the car park.

I glance back. The big car's still sitting in front of the house. It hasn't moved. I wonder if he needs to make an excuse to go out.

"I reckon it could take us an hour to get back. If we jog."

"An hour?" I say. "We need to do it in half that time."

The fence is one of those low, metal park-type fences. Easy to climb and while I'm thinking that perhaps we should wait for the bus, or even phone for a taxi, Lucas clambers over and starts stomping over the field away from the house. "Do you think it's safe?" I call after him.

He turns. I can just see him in the purple snow light. "She said reindeer thingies."

I follow and as I do, the gentle snow changes from something lazy and curling to something angry and persistent.

He turns and walks away and the snow does its best to come between us in sheets, stinging my face and collecting on my scarf.

"Hey, wait," I say, breaking into a stumbly trot and shuffling through the snow until I reach him.

"So how did your mum react when you told her about Sebastian?"

"She said I wasn't making any sense, but at least I said it, and I've sent her the photo of the car. If it ever leaves my phone."

He walks on and I struggle to keep up. Something looms out of the snow, snorts and turns away. Reindeer perhaps.

I pull my hood closer and lean forward to push through the blizzard. Lucas is huffing and puffing to my right, so although I can't really see him, I know where he is.

Quite without warning, we crash into a fence. It's tall. Chain-link.

"This must be where we need to find the gate," I shout.

Lucas may say something, but his words are whipped away by the wind.

In the snow, I can barely see him.

"I can't remember which way," I shout, working my way along the fence. I'm now unable to see and I flail with my right hand, reaching into space until at last I grasp something soft and giving.

"Lucas?" I murmur, peering through the snow.

Whatever it is, it coughs at me and jerks its head away. Multiple feet sound on the snow. The reindeer have been disturbed by something.

"Lucas?"

I stop and listen.

I don't know where he is.

"Lucas?"

"LUCAS!"

I've lost him.

He can't be far away so I stop with my back to the fence and look around in a big arc.

The only things I can really see are grey blobs that must be the reindeer. They're snuffling at the ground, presumably looking for grass. Is he among them?

"Lucas!" I bellow.

"LUCAS!"

I'm not really alarmed. More annoyed. This is a waste of time.

Which direction did Jacqui say? Left or right?

I head right. I'm fairly sure Lucas didn't pass me, so maybe he's just ahead.

Keeping the chain-link on my left, I walk up a gentle slope. I can't see very far, and when I look back towards the house it's vanished behind the sheets of snow. It's also definitely trying to get dark now.

The slope gets steeper, and the snow deeper, little crusts cresting over the top of Mum's boots.

I keep going, but soon I'm holding on to the fence just to get up the slope. Through the snow, I can't work out where I am. If I could only see the house.

I stumble up the last little summit and suddenly I'm on a flat area.

Slapping the snow from my gloves I pull out my phone and try texting Lucas.

Where are U?

It takes a moment for him to text back.

Bottom of a hill. Where u?

Top of hill.

There's a long silence while the snow feathers around me, deadening all sound. The reindeer are off doing their own thing now; they must have found something more interesting than me.

Did you turn right?

Yes.

Be with you in a moment.

I open Google Maps. I can see where I am now. Right in the middle of nothing. The snow rustles. Something takes off in the trees. Something sniffs, stamps its feet.

My back turned to the fence, I look down the hill to the right, waiting for Lucas to emerge from the blizzard.

"C'mon, Lucas," I say out loud. "C'mon."

The fence vibrates to my right and the snow pings off. I peer through the blizzard.

"Here! I'm here," he says.

"C'mon, we've lost loads of time."

"Sorry – I thought she said left. It was Sebastian who said left, wasn't it? Look, this is impossible. I'm going to ring Dad."

He gets out his phone and calls Paolo. I hear him answer and nearly weep.

"Papa!" Lucas talks fast and in Italian and I try hard to follow the conversation. He mentions me and Jacqui and *nonna*, which I think is "Granny" – but I can hear that Paolo isn't taking him seriously. He breaks back into English. "But, Papa, we need your help. You must go to Grandma's. She is in danger!"

And I hear Paolo's response: "No, you're imagining things. Jacqui's rung Sally. If you go back to the house, she'll give you a lift. Stop panicking."

And then the reception goes.

Neither of us speak.

Ahead of me the snow begins to play tricks. It forms into blobs and then away again.

And then something really close howls. Twice.

Chapter 20

"Wolves," whispers Lucas. "He's released the wolves."

I stop. Still. Isn't that what the man said? Stay still.

And I listen.

The snow has changed to small, sharp, driving needles. They bounce from my nose and sting my eyes. The wolves don't seem to mind. They're just waiting.

I stand as still as I can.

Lucas moves slightly closer to me.

We can do this.

Can't we?

"Sing," he says.

"Hm?"

"Sing. Sing to them. The man said it."

"That was lions."

"Was it?"

"I still think we should try."

"Why don't you?"

"You're better at it."

"D'you think wolves like *Hairspray*?" I whisper.

"They might."

I open my mouth and sing, "Good morning..." My voice almost dies, but I keep it up. Thin and reedy, the words seem to stop dead in the air, brought down by the snow. I get to the end of the line and I'm about to stop and yell for help when another voice joins mine, much more confident, deep and warm. It's Lucas, and he knows all the words.

Together we reach the end of the next line and we're joined by a wolf. A long howl that makes my blood freeze and brings on the howling of the rest of the pack.

Two, three, six, and I lose count. They're all doing it.

Are we that bad?

We shuffle along the fence, our backs to it, singing as we make our way hopefully across the flat patch. At times, Lucas's voice booms and the wolves follow. They're interested in us but they don't actually approach, they merely howl – out of disgust or fascination I've no idea.

Distantly, I hear a car.

Definitely the roar of an engine, and it doesn't sound like the slow tourist cars making their way up the drive.

The roar gets louder.

"Yay, the gate," sings Lucas. "Right there!"

"You're kidding," I sing in reply.

"Key in the numbers," he chants.

"Will do." I key one-nine-five-four into the keypad and the doors slide slowly open. Really wide. Our arms linked, we slowly back through. One of the wolves follows us, but the gate begins to close and at the last second he panics and runs back to the pack.

We drop the singing and I very nearly collapse.

"Whoa," I say, resting my hands on my knees and waiting for my breathing to get back under control.

Lucas doesn't say anything, just breathes in and out like he's never tasted oxygen before.

On the other side of the gate the wolves melt away and we take a moment to look at our surroundings.

Yellow headlight beams light the strings of snow falling through the trees. "That car's close," says Lucas.

"I don't like it," I say, glancing back. "Let's get down to the main road."

"I reckon there's a track if we could only see it," says Lucas, stumbling across the ground. "Oh no, look, more gates. This must be a kind of holding area."

As we crunch through the snow towards another set of gates, giant headlights floodlight the trees.

"Quick," I say. "Do the code."

Ahead of me Lucas jabs at the keypad. The gates in front of us roll slowly open, but the ones behind us remain closed.

"Hey!" shouts a voice behind us. Sebastian?

"It's like a canal lock," says Lucas, tugging at my

sleeve, and we begin to run long before the gates open all the way. "You can't have both sides open at once."

"Stop – stop! Ruby!" It's definitely Sebastian. He says something else, but we're too far ahead to hear.

"Keep going," I shout.

Lucas doesn't answer, instead he lowers his head and hurtles forward into the trees. I chase behind him, listening for the clang of the gates closing, Thank goodness they're taking their time. The snow's falling so thickly we just need to get ourselves into the trees, out of sight. Sebastian'll never find us there. Lucas charges through some pines, thwacking into the branches and pinging them back in my face. "Sorry!" he shouts. I lower my head and charge until I'm running parallel with him.

"Are we going in the right direction?" he pants.

I pull my phone out of my pocket and flip on the screen. Our little blue dot is closer to the road, I think, and as I watch, we move closer still. "Still quite a long way though."

"Stop a sec," says Lucas. "Got a stitch."

I drop to a crouch. All around us the snow

scuffles and snuffles at the branches. It's falling thickly again, but here in the trees it's silent.

I hear a distant clang. "The gates closing, I think," I say.

Beside me Lucas crouches and in the gloom I see him take his inhaler out of his pocket and take a couple of deep breaths. Then he coughs and spits to the side. "Sorry," he says. "I had to stop."

"OK?" I ask, aware that somewhere behind us is Sebastian. Either inside or outside the gates. The only good thing about that is that if he's chasing us, he's not going to Granny's to look for the evidence.

"What are we waiting for?" Lucas sets off and I stay close beside him. The ground is uneven, so we stumble. There are trees to the right, and every now and again they drop tons of snow, making a flump sound that makes me jump.

We walk on in silence.

As we walk, I begin to feel the movement of something else. We're not the only people in this landscape. Someone else is here.

But how could Sebastian have got so close so fast? So silently.

I touch Lucas's sleeve.

"Stop," I whisper.

He stops.

Whoever is following us also stops.

But I can hear breathing.

Heavy, old-man breathing.

I step out, moving a little faster, risking a glance at my phone searching for our blue dot on the map. We don't seem to have got any closer to the road but whatever was behind us is now beside us. On both sides.

The breathing is coming from everywhere. Three old men? Three old men rumbly-breathing and not talking?

I look to the side. I can't see anyone there – nor past Lucas.

It's not Lucas. His breathing comes with a whistle. This is kind of deep and snotty. Someone with a giant nose.

And I can hear the snow crunching under someone's feet.

"What's the matter?" whispers Lucas.

"Someone there," I murmur.

We walk on. I hope we're still heading in the right direction. Every one of our steps is matched by the invisible snow crunching alongside us.

"I don't think it's Sebastian."

"I think we should run."

"'K," says Lucas. "Go!"

He leaps away, heading into the woods and as he does, I see the invisible stalkers. Four of them.

Lions.

Chapter 21

I'm frozen.

We mustn't run. Aren't we supposed to make ourselves big?

Oh – what was it that keeper said at the wedding?

Flump.

Something whizzes past my ear.

Oh, pants, he's shooting at us now.

Flump.

A tufted thing hits a tree in front of me, vibrating as it's stopped by the wood.

Darts. He's shooting darts at us.

Stuff that would bring down a lion. Or kill a person.

It's fight or flight, and my flight instinct cuts in. I run. I run through the lions, except now there are two. Where are the other two?

I don't care – I just want to stay alive.

"Lucas!" I shout.

Flump.

This arrow comes from a different direction and passes within a centimetre of my ear.

"Here!" Lucas yells from far ahead.

Underneath me the ground's uneven and I stumble again and again. My gloves are wet with pushing myself off trees and up from the ground.

Something's galloping alongside me and it isn't Lucas.

Run!

Flump.

Another dart hits a tree.

I dodge left, dodge right, hurdle a tree trunk and land knee-deep in squidgy snow-covered leaves on the other side.

I can't hear Lucas any more.

The galloping thing races to my right. It's cutting

me off, separating us.

Flump.

I kick down and run on, my lungs screaming, my legs burning.

Left, right, left – down, down.

I crash through a line of bushes into more woods, lit this time by a distant yellow lamp. I swing myself towards it.

I don't know if I'm being shot at. I don't know if there are any lions. I don't know where Lucas is. I just keep running – my lungs bursting, the air so cold, the snow so cold. Branches whip my face, my boots fill with ice, my pockets tear as I catch them on the brambles. Downhill. Downhill – I have to get to the bottom. I have to get to the lamp.

I kick down and race towards the lamp.

The lamp on the other side of the fence.

Sucking in the air, I turn my back to the fence and face uphill. If I'm going to be killed by a dart, I want to face Sebastian. And if by a lion – I want to see its teeth.

But there's nothing. No one. Just the woods in the snow. It might as well be Narnia.

My heart's still hammering in my chest and even

though I'm taking the deepest breaths, I'm still gasping for air.

What's happened? Where's Lucas?

I reach into my pocket, slowly, slowly. I don't want to make any sudden moves in case there's a lion nearby.

I close my hand on air.

No phone.

I reach into the other pocket, but I can tell by the sinking feeling in my stomach that I know it's not going to be there.

I pat my jeans, search my pockets again and, for the first time, feel like giving up.

I may only be a mile from my granny's, but I'm stuck in a lion pen with someone shooting at me. I've lost my Step and I've lost my phone.

Just to make it more hopeless, I'm caught out by sudden tears and I have to sniff them back, making an awful loud snorting.

"Come on, Ruby," I mutter. "If you can deal with wolves you can deal with lions."

The singing worked.

I think.

I edge into "Good Morning Baltimore", so

quietly I can hardly hear it, but it steadies my breathing and it does give me more courage.

The street lamp on the other side is actually a light next to a tall signal box thing. Probably what the keepers use to keep an eye on the lions. The box has blank windows and a closed door and is on the other side of a chain-link fence. I wave, in case there's someone watching on a CCTV camera, but they will all have gone home for the day by now. There's no point hanging around waiting for help.

I put my right shoulder to the fence and begin to walk along the side of it, looking up every so often in the hope it's become shorter. It hasn't. I run out of "Good Morning Baltimore" and try "I Can Hear the Bells". I wish I could hear the bells. It would be so comforting.

Where's Lucas?

The fence goes on for ages. And ages. It climbs up and to the left and I suspect I may be going the whole way round, back to the gate I came through, when I find another tall gate.

I peer at the snow. There's snow light but all the daylight's gone and it's hard to see, but I'm pretty sure there aren't any footprints. Human or lion.

The gate's another one operated by a touch pad. Should I go through? Or will I end up in with the tigers?

I stand for a moment listening to the snow, and then I hear cars, on a road.

So this can't be the tigers — can it? I'm too close to the main road, surely.

I type one-nine-five-four into the keypad and the gates rumble open.

It's another lock. I stand in the middle, between the gates, under a closed-down sentry box, and wait for the other gate to open.

I could stay here. Until light. I might freeze to death, but I wouldn't be eaten alive. My fingers hover over the keypad. I could just shut both gates.

And leave Lucas to his fate.

"Lucas!" I shout.

"LUCAS!"

There's no answer.

The gate in front of me opens and I step out.

There's a small field. And I can see through the snow that there are sheep in it. I can actually hear them chewing.

I let my breath go and my heartbeat steadies.

I can do this. A sheep field. The main road. Down to the canal and up the other side.

I look back into the lion enclosure. Nothing's moving. No one's there. I haven't heard a dart, or a roar, or a footstep.

"Lucas!" I shout as loud as I can.

"LUCAS!" A bird wakes and leaps from a branch, and snow tumbles to the ground, snapping twigs as it falls, but no one shouts back.

"Where are you, Lucas?" I say to the trees.

And the trees stay silent.

The sheep follow me, all of us crunching through the snow until I am back by another fence, this one made of three easily climbed iron bars. I stop and look back. There is no sign of anyone else in this landscape. The best I can do for Lucas now is to get help.

I step over and leave the sheep to their chewing.

The ground falls away on the far side of the field. It's steep and the snow has fallen in a thick carpet here. With no trees to grip on to and the ground sliding away beneath my feet, I sit on my bum and shuffle down the slope. It's too steep and I'm too slow. I stand and look right and left. There are some pheasant feeders dotted along the top, just below the fence. This must be where the shoot happens. I shiver. Glad they don't fire in the dark.

I shuffle along, sliding a little and posting more snow over the top of my boots until I reach the nearest feeder. The top is a circle of plastic. Like a bin lid. Gripping it on both sides, I sit down and push with my legs. I don't mean to push much, but the lid has other ideas and skates smoothly over the snow, bouncing me down the slope, gaining speed.

Last time I went sledging I seem to remember that pulling up the front slows you down, but the lid doesn't know that rule and I begin to hurtle, leaving the ground from time to time and bouncing on, faster and faster, so fast that I begin to wonder about the road at the bottom.

The lid has no intention of stopping and my fingers are frozen gripping the front. I could let go but I might fly head first. I pass a tree, then another, and a set of headlights cross in front of me. Less than a second later I'm on a small cliff above the road. There's a car – lights. I grip the lid, close my eyes and shoot off the cliff on to the hard surface of the road.

Toooooooot!

Tooooot!

The car skids.

I see the tyres, the lights, but I'm moving so fast that I whisk straight over and off the other side.

"Sorry!" I shout, as me and my sledge crash on down, through a bramble, whipped by small branches and bumped by boulders until I see the canal below me.

Oh no.

Ice.

I grip tighter and wait for the shock of the icy water.

Chapter 22

Crack.

The lid breaks.

The ice cracks.

But I stay on top, sliding on my knees, slowed by the inches of snow, frightening a duck. Dry.

I stop, and try to stand. Underneath the snow is ice. It's slippery and, although it's thick I can hear the ominous sound of cracks racing across the surface.

Lying flat, I paddle myself to the side and clamber up through the frozen grasses, grasping something hanging over that turns out to be a stinging nettle. I've escaped lions. Escaped lions!

My hands are frozen. My boots full of snow. But I let myself smile.

"Hello! Hello!" a voice calls from above me. "Ruby? Is that you?"

I stand and look up at where I shot through the bushes on the main road.

There's a figure standing there, backlit by headlights.

It's not Lucas.

"Hello!" I call back. "I'm really sorry, but who is that?"

"It's me, Anthony. I thought it was you – I saw your red coat shoot across the road in front of me."

"Oh, Anthony!"

"Do you want a lift? I reckon I can just about get up the hill."

I waddle over the frozen canal and pull myself up the bank on the far side. The snow has flattened where I came through, and it takes a helping hand from Anthony and some inelegant hedge-tangling from me and then I'm standing on the main road, staring at his car. It's a substantial four-wheel drive. Not as large as Sebastian's, but big enough to make short work of the snow. Quite suddenly, I feel like crying. I'd never thought of Anthony as a saviour, but here he is with a big, warm, safe car.

"Jump in," he says. "What are you doing here?"

"Avoiding the lions."

I climb up into the passenger seat. It's all very tech and smells of Jacqui's perfume.

"What?" says Anthony. "The lions? How did you end up in there?"

"We were visiting your mum and she told us to go right to get out of the park. I think she must have meant left. I was with Lucas, but somehow we got separated. I'm really worried about him."

"We'll get help. No signal here. But I'm sure he's fine." Anthony's driving along the main road as if the snow wasn't bucketing down. I guess in a car like this it doesn't make much odds. We go over a bump and something in the back of the car clangs. He starts talking again. "Mum's always getting her left and right muddled up. You must have been terrified. I'm amazed you're still alive. What did you go to the safari park for?"

I stare out the window, listening to the curious rhythms that the car and the snow are making. There's music, but there's another rhythmic thump. It seems to be coming from the boot. Odd. It's as if there's someone in there.

"We went to talk to your mum."

"About what?" asks Anthony.

"I don't know whether I should say."

Anthony stays silent, and in the end I speak just to fill the gap.

"I wanted to talk to her about Dr Price's murder and all the weird stuff that's been going on recently. I told her that there was a piece of evidence that Lucas and I found near Dr Price's body, one that pointed to the safari park, or, more particularly, Sebastian."

"Oh?" asks Anthony.

"I found a sort of charm – a gross charm, admittedly – on the side of the road near where we found Dr Price, and Lucas found a picture of Sebastian's first wife wearing it, as part of a necklace. And we found a letter, to Dr Price. About poisons."

Anthony brakes to avoid a rabbit.

"So what are you saying? Are you saying that

231

Sebastian is ... a murderer?"

"I am — I really am. I tried telling Jacqui earlier but she said she was one hundred per cent certain that Sebastian couldn't be — but I'm not so sure. I think your mother might be in danger, Anthony. I know it sounds crazy but you should know so you can try to keep her safe."

Under the trees the snow is thinner, but the road is still empty.

Anthony doesn't say anything for a long time.

"I think," he says, "you might be right."

Chapter 23

We drive slowly along the main road, down towards the traffic lights. I turn to look into the back in case I can see somebody in there. I glance at the seat behind me. It seems to be full of equipment; pipes and cables and things that are probably techy parts of Anthony's work. Also a load of red fluffy feathered things. I can't imagine what they're for.

"Scary about the lions," he says. "Did they chase you?"

"Not exactly. In fact, they were less scary than—" I pause. Then I turn round to look at the back seat again. Those red fluffy things look awfully like the things that were flying through the air when I was running from the lions. Darts.

"Than what?" Anthony asks, swinging the car into the road that goes towards Granny's.

Which is interesting, because I haven't mentioned going to Granny's.

And I have an unwanted thought.

How did he know I have a red coat?

Unless.

The man in the market. He was tall, like Anthony.

I babble. "So it's really lovely in the snow, isn't it? I love the way the countryside looks — even the electricity substation is attractive in this…"

I always babble when I'm nervous, and as I'm babbling, I think.

All of this points to Anthony. He's driving his own car now — but he could have driven Sebastian's. Sebastian could have lost his keys because Anthony had them. Anthony drives a car — uses computers — knows his way around the surgery. He works on phone-tapping technology — so he could have listened to all the conversations and he would have known Dr Price. He had every reason to help

Sebastian's wife to die. The sooner she died, the sooner his mother could marry him.

"... it must be really brilliant to be able to drive this car – four-wheel drive and that. Did you know we're doing *Hairspray* next week? Lucas is playing a big part, which will be really..."

As my words spout, I go on thinking. Jacqui can't possibly know about it. It must be Anthony on his own.

And now I'm in his car.

"I hope Lucas is OK. You didn't see him through the snow?"

"No," he says. "But we can use a call box at the top of the hill."

I'm pretty sure I now know where Lucas is. And it's not on a snowy hillside being eaten by lions, thank goodness; it's hiding in the boot of this car. He would have been down to my right. He must have reached the chain-link fence with the lamppost on the other side and he would have been able to climb it. He'd have reached the main road before me. Anthony would have driven past him, before I shot across the road. And Lucas would have worked Anthony out before I did.

He's stowed away and those thumps are him telling me he's there.

In the darkness of the car, I reach for the door handle. It's cold under my fingers and I give it a little tug. Nothing moves. Childlock? It's almost certainly the kind of car where the boot doesn't open from the inside. Lucas has climbed in, but he may not be able to climb out.

Anthony turns the car around the long bends and we creep along the road, heading for the railway bridge at the bottom of the hill.

I stop babbling and relax a little as we climb the hill. Halfway, there's a car across the road.

"Oh, look, this is fine. I can walk from here," I say, trying to work out how I can release Lucas. "Really, you've done enough."

"No, I think I can get past."

"Really?" I say, as he skilfully manoeuvres the car on and off the pavement to the left and just skims by.

I'm desperately trying to come up with an excuse to get out of the car. I could be suddenly sick. Or a nosebleed – not that I have nosebleeds. I could faint. What good would that do?

We're nearly at the top of the hill. From here, I could run over the fields, I could get to Granny's before him.

"Oh – shoot!" he says.

There, miraculously jammed across the road, is the bus. Windows lit up; passengers still inside. It must have got stuck ages ago because there's a breakdown truck on the far side.

"What a shame," says Anthony. "I really thought I could get you there."

"Oh well, no matter. I can get to Granny's from here really easily, honestly. I can call for help now."

"I'll come with you. You must be shaken after that tumble across the road." He reaches into the back for something. It gleams. A gun?

"Um – well, OK," I say. "Although Granny doesn't much welcome callers."

"I won't come in, just see you to the door. Mum wouldn't forgive me for leaving you out here on your own."

The doors click open and I step down.

Now what am I going to do? And how am I going to get Lucas out?

Chapter 24

The moment I step out of the car, Anthony is there next to me. He nudges me round to the front, grabbing his jacket from the back seat by shoving me forward.

I start walking immediately. Leaving him to run to catch up. I'm furiously thinking as I stomp.

Lucas is in the boot of that car.

I need an excuse.

I know.

I pat my pockets.

"Oh no, I've left my phone in the car."

"I'll get it," says Anthony.

"No — I will, it's fine."

"I'll come with you,"

We walk back together. I gabble and babble and fill the air with stupid talk. I hope Lucas can hear this.

"It must be in the front somewhere," I say.

We get right up to the side of the car before he twings the beeper and the doors open. I climb up to look in the front passenger seat. "Oh — there it is," I say, leaning right over the seat, my legs sticking out. "I just can't — can't quite, oh!"

"What's the matter?" he asks.

"It's over the far side, jammed between the seat and the handbrake thingy in the middle. You might have better luck," I say.

"Let me look." He clambers on to the door sill and leans right over.

"It should be there, right there," I say, running around to the back of the car and clicking the boot open.

Lucas rises up like the undead, and I run back to the front of the car where Anthony is still leaning over.

I hear a soft flump as Lucas leaps from the boot, closes it with a barely audible click – thank goodness – and scuttles out of sight.

"Can you see it? It's black."

I'm tempted to slam the door on him, but I reckon if I can delay him for a while, Lucas should be able to get to Granny's.

What he'll do when he gets there I don't know.

Ring the police?

Turn Grandpa's fossil collection into missiles?

"Can't find it," says Anthony, jerking backward and banging his head on the roof.

"Oh – perhaps I lost it in the park," I say, theatrically patting my pockets.

"Perhaps you did," he says.

The passengers from the bus have been loaded into a minibus and I speed up, hoping to get to them before they leave, but they pull away a moment before I reach them. I still manage to waste a few minutes examining the state of the bus and pointing out the skid marks on the ground.

The snow has stopped and it's very quiet up here except for the low whistle of the wind and the sound of a dog barking somewhere.

"Come on," says Anthony. "Let's get going. You need to tell someone about Lucas and I should get back to Ma and Sebastian."

We turn from the main road into the village, passing a bus stop and a freshly sprayed owl tag.

Good. He's ahead of us.

I stroll, I wander, I make footprints, I throw an experimental snowball, all waiting for the moment at which Anthony snaps and the threat moves from deep and low to on the surface. I stop to admire the sky – it's clearing now and the moon is showing between the clouds... Small snowfalls cascade from the trees.

He doesn't snap and I manage to waste about ten minutes. Ten minutes that should have allowed Lucas to get there, and explain.

Granny's house is beyond the church, and I dawdle past, pointing out the pretty ledges of snow on the churchyard walls, and not pointing out the new stencilled owl on the corner of the noticeboard.

Anthony says nothing, and I realise that he doesn't know where she lives.

A woman comes past walking a dog. "Evening,"

she says. "Lovely, isn't it? Snow day tomorrow."

"Yes," I say, wondering if I should flag her down and try and explain – but what good would it do? Anthony's right there, and I'm pretty sure he's holding a gun. "Sledging," I say. We pass the Seven Stars, windows glowing to the right, and the Social Club on my left. Here the houses thin. I can see Granny's.

Beyond her house is the swimming lake.

And I have an idea.

Chapter 25

Yellow squares show in the kitchen window of Granny's house. And there's more than one person inside.

Lucas.

He made it.

My dread notches down a gear and I take a long, deep breath.

And then just down the road, I see the big car.

Sebastian's.

What?

But I haven't got time to think.

I knock on Granny's door, push it open and almost suffocate in the warm fug.

"Hello!" I call out cheerily.

"In the kitchen," shouts a voice.

It's not Granny.

Anthony comes in behind me.

"Thank you for the lift," I say. "That's really kind."

He ignores me, brushing past all the walking aids, sending them clattering to the floor. "Ma?" he shouts. "Oh! And you."

My head turns the corner into the kitchen and I see Jacqui, Granny and Lucas sitting around the table. Granny meets my eye and raises her eyebrow but she doesn't say anything.

Lucas is sheet-white and he's glaring at me. I wonder what that glare means.

"Hello, darling," says Jacqui. "I was so worried about you, thought I'd find you on the way — came to check you were all tickety-boo. And — what you said, it's been bothering me…"

Dry-mouthed, I creak a garbled, "Oh."

I'm behind Anthony.

"Pop and get the charm, show me," says Jacqui.

"I really need proof that I've married a murderer!" She puts her hand over her mouth and giggles, and at that moment I let all my doubts flood in and I see right through her and all the lies she's spun.

I want to sit down. I want to discuss this with Lucas and Granny but instead I say, "Oh, OK. Put the kettle on. I must use the bathroom and then I'll dig it out. It's upstairs."

Before anyone can stop me I clatter past the walkers into Granny's downstairs loo, lock the door behind me and open the window above the toilet itself. It's just big enough, I reckon.

It takes a moment for me, my boots and my coat to bundle through.

I'm in her garden. Behind it is a field, with the swimming lake.

This'll never work.

Yes, it will.

I run to the back window of the kitchen and tap on it, waving frantically. Lucas's eyes go wide. I leg it across the garden, straight over Granny's frozen pond, jumping over the small box hedges and crashing through the raspberry canes until I reach the fence at the bottom. I turn for a second to see Anthony and Jacqui standing in the back doorway of the cottage, peering out into the dark.

The fence is three strands of barbed wire. I duck through the gap in the middle, like I've done a thousand times when taking sneaky swims in the private lake on a hot summer's evening. When I'm safely on the other side I turn and look back again. Black figures bob in front of the glow from the house. I can't tell how close they are but now's the time to run. I break into a jog, and then push myself to properly run. Ahead, I can see a lamp that must be on the swimmer's hut on the far side. Sprinting towards the light, I only slow for the slope that goes down to the lake itself. Underfoot is solid, it will be all the way around the sides, but there's a stream that runs in from the right-hand side – there's no way the ice can freeze thickly across the middle. At least, I hope not.

I stop to get my breath. I need to go close enough to the middle to tempt them, but far enough away not to fall through. Above me, the clouds break again and the moonlight floods through, lighting up the whole field. The huge lake shows as a circular shadow and I'm just inside the circle. Behind me,

Jacqui shouts to Anthony, "There she is, get her!"

I was right.

Resisting the impulse to run, I walk straight ahead, until the snow crunch turns to ice crack.

Then I swing left, and a couple of metres inside the edge of the ice begin to run again. This is the deep end of the lake – not that deep, but deep enough. There'll be things asleep under the ice.

I risk running closer to the middle.

Crack.

A cloud covers the moon and the light drops.

Brilliant timing.

Under cover of darkness I head back for the shoreline.

"OW!" comes a shout. Anthony on the barbed wire.

I'm nearly round the lake. Just a little further and I can stop on the far side.

I can't ring the police; I don't have a phone. I can only hope that Lucas has done it. Or that Granny has done it, or a fish at the bottom of the lake has done it.

This is mad.

I so hope this works.

The light on the swimmer's hut is quite clear now and I head towards it, stopping beneath it so that my red coat shows up.

I wave.

And I wait, and I watch.

The moon comes out and I hope that my footsteps are hidden in the lumps and tussocks of the field. I hope that it looks as if I've run in a roughly straight line.

Two figures appear at the far side of the lake.

I really, really hope that Jacqui doesn't know about the lake.

It was only dug the year before last.

If it doesn't work, I'm going to have to break into the cricket club and run over their pitch and get all the way back round.

"I've got it in my pocket!" I shout.

"What?"

"Here! In my pocket – come and get it!"

Turning away, although I'm desperate to see what's happening, I run across the rest of the field towards the cricket club.

Ahead of me is untouched snow, although I know there's a ditch, which will hopefully be frozen, and a line of stinging nettles.

I'm jogging more than running when I hear the shout.

"No! Anthony, you can't do that. It's Ruby!"

There's the sharp crack of a shot.

"Oh no!"

"Anthony!"

"Mum!"

I can't bear it, I have to look.

There in the middle of the depression are the two figures. Clinging to each other. One tall, one shorter.

And I can hear something like distant lightning, moving from one side to the other. Soft, repeating, deadly. The surface of the ice crazing, giving way. Groaning, crunching ice.

The taller one breaks and runs towards me, the shorter one drops to her hands and knees.

I watch until they both fall through the ice.

Chapter 26

It takes a while for the police to come. In the meantime, with the whole village watching, Granny's neighbour Mr Twissell, who used to be a policeman, gets his small vintage tractor out and drives into the lake to rescue Anthony and Jacqui. It turns out that when Anthony fired the gun, he shot the ice and dropped the gun. Just as well really.

If he hadn't, they might have got to me.

While Lucas, Granny and I watch from the side, she cuddles us both and says things like "Chip off the old block – your grandpa brought a mugger down with his walking stick in nineteen eighty-six," and "Not how I expected today to turn out."

Granny, the vicar and Mr Twissell lock Anthony and Jacqui in his garage, without the tractor but with blankets and a heater. Honestly, they don't need locking up, they're frozen solid, but Granny says she won't have them in the house, and Mr Twissell says he doesn't fancy them in his house either.

"But I don't want to be responsible for their deaths from hypothermia."

We stand in the garden wrapped in doggy blankets listening to Anthony shouting and Jacqui telling him to shut up.

"Are you OK?" I ask Lucas.

"Amazingly, yes," he says. "I was so worried about you – I thought you'd been eaten by the lions."

"I thought *you* had," I say. "And then Anthony picked me up. He must have been patrolling the edge of the woods."

"Yeah, I saw that and climbed in when he was helping you up from the canal, and then I thought I'd be stuck in there forever."

"I heard you, but it took me a while to work it

out. How did you get through the lions?"

"Someone was firing darts at them; I saw one go down. At first I thought they were firing at me, but then I realised that they were keeping me safe. Then I climbed the fence."

"All terrifying," says Granny. "And then the dear boy fetches up on my doorstep. I rang the police a second before Jacqui appeared. It was all terribly awkward – I have to confess I began to babble," Granny laughs. "Not had such verbal diarrhoea for years!"

Blue lights bounce from the snow and Granny goes back into the house to answer the door.

"I really did think you were dead," I say.

"And you, little Step," says Lucas, dropping his doggy blanket and reaching his long, awkward arms around me. It's nice. I like it. A brotherly hug, my first one.

The police take Jacqui and Anthony off in a van with space blankets and dry clothes.

And they ask us a billion questions. We sit next to each other on Granny's front-room sofa with Donald and the exercise bike.

"So where is this piece of evidence?" It's a new police officer, a woman. Older, grumpier. "And really it wasn't up to you – you should have called us."

I'm going to let it slide, but Lucas obviously isn't. "We brought the tooth to you and you said it wasn't important – you'll find a record of it somewhere. And then when our car was rammed nobody came! Honestly, why would we go to the police? And you've been chasing after Oskar, who isn't – who didn't – who couldn't possibly…"

He's bright red. Anger or embarrassment, I'm not sure, but I feel inexplicably proud of him.

"And there's a letter – a toxicology report. Only…"

"Only what?"

"I can't find it," says Lucas.

"We can't find it," I join in.

"Let me get this right." The grumpy police officer frowns at us. "You say Sebastian Duncan's first wife died in suspicious circumstances? Was murdered – so that Jacqueline could marry him?"

I nod. Lucas nods. We nod at each other.

"And this Dr Price was suspicious, confronted

Jacqueline and was killed himself?"

"Yes, by Anthony, or by both of them. They left him on the side of Brassknocker Hill."

"In a box."

"Which we opened."

"In the snow."

"But we found the tooth from the necklace – the necklace that Sebastian gave his first wife, and then gave to Jacqui."

"Which she lost when she and Anthony were disposing of the body."

"And then, we found…"

"Discovered…"

"Came across…"

"The toxicology report."

The police officer rubs her forehead and asks us to start again.

Granny's in her element, offering cups of tea to the police team, who are examining the big car outside and talking to each other on walkie-talkies clipped to their stab vests.

I phone Mum, who rings off immediately so that she can call Paolo and a taxi.

Paolo calls Granny, who tells him to walk up the

hill because the road's blocked.

For a while there's a lot of activity and not many questions, and in the warm, wearing Granny's slippers and drinking her lapsang souchong tea (faintly disgusting – try it), I begin to doze. It's OK now. All of it. And it all makes sense.

As if he can read my mind, Lucas says, "Dead dogs. The fraud was a dead dog."

"Dead cat," says Granny.

"What?" I ask.

"A distraction. We were given something to take us off the scent. The money, missing from the surgery. It might be Jacqui was stealing it – it might be that Oskar found it out – but what it did was to make us think that the crime was solved." He stares at a photo of one of Donald's predecessors. "Or it made the police feel that way."

"And Mum," I say. "And Paolo."

"But I was never convinced," he says, staring into space.

"It was me that wasn't convinced," I say, poking him.

He laughs. "I know. And if you hadn't kept going, hadn't worried at it – we'd never have found out the truth."

"What about Sebastian? What's happened to him? Granny, do you know?"

"I don't," she says, rushing out through the door to collar one of the policemen. "Excuse me, excuse me!"

But we don't find out because they want me to show them where Anthony's car is. They can't find it.

Borrowing Granny's wellies and putting on my red coat, I stomp over the snow towards the road. There's a man in a white paper suit who follows me, and a young police officer in ordinary clothes who shines her torch everywhere and talks to me as if I was six. I don't really care, although we don't need the torch – the moon's doing all the work and the fields are thick with new snow. We reach the car and she uses the blippy thing to open the doors, poking inside with a pen.

"I'll take it from here," says the man in the white paper suit.

"Lucas was in the boot," I say. "And I think Anthony shot at us with those things." I tap the back window, pointing to the darts.

"Don't touch!" they both call.

"Crime scene," says the woman.

"Yeah," I say, thinking it's going to be covered in my fingerprints because I was in there earlier. "Yeah, I know."

Mum and Paolo fetch up soon after we go back into the house and she gives me a massive hug. We all sit for an age in the sitting room with Lucas and Granny and the exercise bike, which is pretty exciting if you're Donald, and cosy if you're the rest of us.

"I don't believe it though," says Mum. "Jacqui? And what's happened to Oskar then?"

Lucas shrugs and then a funny look comes over his face.

"What?" I say.

"Oskar," he says. "I think I might know. I think Anthony might have been talking about it on the phone when I climbed in the back of the car."

"You must tell the police," says Paolo, "if you know anything at all."

"It's just a suspicion." Lucas lets out a long sigh.

"Animals?" I ask.

Lucas nods.

"Tigers."

"Oh, lordy!" says Granny. "That's awful."

"I might be wrong," says Lucas.

Chapter 27

Even though we're taking a day off school, I don't sleep in, and, much to my surprise, when I go downstairs Lucas is already up, sitting chatting to his dad in the kitchen.

"Christmas market today," says Paolo.

"Really?" I ask, looking at Lucas.

"Yup," he smiles. "And then pizza at the Real Italian."

We go in on the bus, which creeps slowly into town, passing the picture-postcard valley and sloshing in through the slush on the edge of town.

The market looks beautiful. The little wooden chalets have snow on their roofs and some of them have huge icicles dangling from the corners. It's bitterly cold, but I don't care and Paolo buys us hot dogs and Mum buys us spiced apple juice.

"I'm sorry Granny didn't come," I say.

"She's got some online Scrabble championship," Mum says. "Can't possibly miss it, and I think she's managed to persuade one of the policemen to join in."

"She would!" says Lucas.

We laugh and eat, and eat again, and all of yesterday seems like a dream.

"Oh," says Mum, cramming a chunk of gorgonzola into her mouth. "Sebastian. I've got a text."

"And?"

Mum chews and scrolls through her phone, making irritating little oohs and aahs.

"Gosh," she says. "I didn't know about the lions. You never told me that..." She frowns and Paolo leans forward across the table.

"Lions?"

"Um..." I shrug. "We were OK though."

Mum purses her lips and snorts. "Well, we can come to lions later, but this is from Sebastian, who has obviously had a very difficult time with the police going over everything – and everyone. But he's asking if you were all right? He says: *I last saw Ruby running through the trees. I do hope she got out OK. I downed all four of the lions. They're fine, it was a low dose, just enough to make them woozy. But I was worried and what on earth was she doing in there?*"

I sit back. "That explains it."

"What does it explain?" asks Paolo, pulling a string of mozzarella from his chin.

"I thought I was being fired at – and actually, I think I was, but the darts came very quickly and from more than one direction."

"I thought that too," says Lucas. "So it was Sebastian?"

"And Anthony – except that Anthony *was* firing at us."

"But not such a good shot as Sebastian," says Lucas.

"I think he saved us," I say. "And we thought he was capable of such terrible things."

"And we thought Oskar was, and he's…" Mum

stops, tears in her eyes.

"Exactly," says Paolo. "We jumped to conclusions. Just because you'd known Jacqui for so many years, and Anthony for all of his life didn't mean that he wasn't a criminal."

Mum blows her nose and sighs.

Stuffed with pizza, we clamber back on the bus and bumble home through the half-dark.

Mum and Paolo settle on the sofa to watch an obscure Russian movie, which I know means that Mum's in a good state because she can't deal with that stuff usually. I wonder how she feels though. Jacqui is – or was – her very best friend. And Oskar.

They still haven't found Oskar.

"The performance is on Wednesday," says Lucas.

"It is," I reply, wondering what he's going to say.

"I wondered…"

I wait.

"I wondered…"

He's finding this hard, and I'd jump in if I wasn't scared I was about to say the wrong thing.

"Would you – could you…?"

"He wants help!" shouts Paolo from the other

side of the room.

"Shut up, Dad!"

"Do you want to go through it, go through *Hairspray* – the dances and all of it?"

Lucas nods his head.

So we do.

Paolo and Mum push the sofas to the side and whisk the coffee table into the kitchen and then politely disappear upstairs, giving us the living room to rehearse.

We do the whole thing – from the beginning to the bitter end. We stop every time Lucas gets it wrong and we do it twice.

Admittedly we have to sing along to the soundtrack, but that's better than nothing, and by the end of it Lucas is good. I never thought I'd say it, but he is – really good.

We go into school the next day and it would be normal except that DS Afolabi comes to talk to us. We get to go in the headteacher's office and the only person who knows what's going on is Mia, and she says nothing. I can see that not knowing is eating up Trixie Thompson, but "Too bad," I say to myself, feeling the excitement of the coming rehearsal and the absolute blinder that I'm hoping Lucas will deliver.

I am actually holding my breath when the dress rehearsal kicks off and Lucas swings on, pops his cuffs and does the whole Corny Collins shebang.

Trixie's jaw almost disconnects from the rest of her head.

"Yes!" says Mia.

Desta's back in school. She watches him and a long, slow smile stretches over her face.

She spots me and comes over holding out an envelope. "I picked it up last week – by accident. I think it's yours?"

My mouth falls open. It's the toxicology report. In the green butterfly envelope with my name on the front. "Yes," I say.

Lucas comes off stage and heads towards me and Mia, but I flick my eyes across to Desta, once, twice, three times before he gets the message and swings round, landing in the seat next to her.

He goes bright red.

Her smile broadens.

Mia and I high-five.

Chapter 28

The night before the performance is Mia's birthday party. Her dad has put a tent in the garden so we don't have to get involved with the skanky dog smells. We eat chocolate and sausages and pizza. We play a sort of hide and seek crossed with murder in the dark – it all ends with a snowball fight. I can't stop screaming and laughing and it feels so brilliantly normal.

When we're settled in sleeping bags with the ice forming in the garden, cosy inside our tent, I tell everyone what happened, but it sounds so odd, so ridiculous that I cut out all the bits about the lions and the wolves. "You had to be there," I say, as I realise that they think I'm making it up.

The day of the performance is the first day we don't see a policeman.

I'm nervous and my stomach is all over the place, but it's not deep dread; more excitement and the feeling that if I ate anything it would come straight up.

Lucas is silent. Mia is determined.

Trixie Thompson is dancing around like a cupcake. So no change there.

We're performing the whole thing in the hall, on a stage that sticks out into the audience so there's the added peril of falling off the stage.

The music starts, and Lucas goes out and absolutely kills it.

When he comes off stage I rush over to hug him, but I'm beaten by Desta. She gives him a kiss – a long, slow, proper on-the-lips kiss.

He goes bright red.

All the coolness deserts him.

He goes from Corny Collins back to Lucas

Mazzotti in less than a second.
   But that's OK.
   He's my Step. And I love him for it.